HORSES NINE

By one desperate leap he shook himself clear. (Page 263.)

HORSES NINE

STORIES OF HARNESS AND SADDLE

BY

SEWELL FORD

ILLUSTRATED

Short Story Index Reprint Series

 BOOKS FOR LIBRARIES PRESS
FREEPORT, NEW YORK

First Published 1903
Reprinted 1970

STANDARD BOOK NUMBER:
8369-3534-9

LIBRARY OF CONGRESS CATALOG CARD NUMBER:
70-122701

PRINTED IN THE UNITED STATES OF AMERICA

CONTENTS

ILLUSTRATIONS

By Frederic Dorr Steele and L. Maynard Dixon

SKIPPER

BEING THE BIOGRAPHY OF A
BLUE-RIBBONER

SKIPPER

BEING THE BIOGRAPHY OF A
BLUE-RIBBONER

AT the age of six Skipper went on the
force. Clean of limb and sound
of wind he was, with not a blemish from
the tip of his black tail to the end of his
crinkly forelock. He had been broken to
saddle by a Green Mountain boy who
knew more of horse nature than of the
trashy things writ in books. He gave
Skipper kind words and an occasional
friendly pat on the flank. So Skipper's
disposition was sweet and his nature a
trusting one.

This is why Skipper learned so soon
the ways of the city. The first time he

saw one of those little wheeled houses, all windows and full of people, come rushing down the street with a fearful whirr and clank of bell, he wanted to bolt. But the man on his back spoke in an easy, calm voice, saying, "So-o-o! There, me b'y. Aisy wid ye. So-o-o!" which was excellent advice, for the queer contrivance whizzed by and did him no harm. In a week he could watch one without even pricking up his ears.

It was strange work Skipper had been brought to the city to do. As a colt he had seen horses dragging ploughs, pulling big loads of hay, and hitched to many kinds of vehicles. He himself had drawn a light buggy and thought it good fun, though you did have to keep your heels down and trot instead of canter. He had liked best to lope off with the boy on his back, down to the Corners, where the store was.

[4]

SKIPPER

But here there were no ploughs, nor hay-carts, nor mowing-machines. There were many heavy wagons, it was true, but these were all drawn by stocky Percherons and big Western grays or stout Canada blacks who seemed fully equal to the task.

Also there were carriages—my, what shiny carriages! And what smart, sleek-looking horses drew them! And how high they did hold their heads and how they did throw their feet about—just as if they were dancing on eggs.

"Proud, stuck-up things," thought Skipper.

It was clear that none of this work was for him. Early on the first morning of his service men in brass-buttoned blue coats came to the stable to feed and rub down the horses. Skipper's man had two names. One was Officer Martin; at least that was the one to which he an-

swered when the man with the cap called
the roll before they rode out for duty.
The other name was "Reddy." That
was what the rest of the men in blue
coats called him. Skipper noticed that
he had red hair and concluded that
"Reddy" must be his real name.

As for Skipper's name, it was written
on the tag tied to the halter which he
wore when he came to the city. Skipper
heard him read it. The boy on the farm
had done that, and Skipper was glad, for
he liked the name.

There was much to learn in those first
few weeks, and Skipper learned it quickly. He came to know that at inspection,
which began the day, you must stand
with your nose just on a line with that of
the horse on either side. If you didn't
you felt the bit or the spurs. He mastered the meaning of "right dress," "left
dress," "forward," "fours right," and a

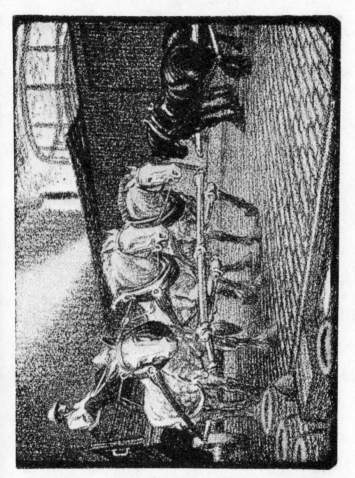

There were many heavy wagons.

lot of other things. Some of them were very strange.

Now on the farm they had said, " Whoa, boy," and " Gid a-a-ap." Here they said, " Halt" and " Forward !" But "Reddy" used none of these terms. He pressed with his knees on your withers, loosened the reins, and made a queer little chirrup when he wanted you to gallop. He let you know when he wanted you to stop, by the lightest pressure on the bit.

It was a lazy work, though. Some-times when Skipper was just aching for a brisk canter he had to pace soberly through the park driveways—for Skipper, although I don't believe I mentioned it before, was part and parcel of the mounted police force. But there, you could know that by the yellow letters on his saddle blanket.

For half an hour at a time he would stand, just on the edge of the roadway

[7]

and at an exact right angle with it, motionless as the horse ridden by the bronze soldier up near the Mall. "Reddy" would sit as still in the saddle, too. It was hard for Skipper to stand there and see those mincing cobs go by, their pad-housings all a-glitter, crests on their blinders, jingling their pole-chains and switching their absurd little stubs of tails. But it was still more tantalizing to watch the saddle-horses canter past in the soft bridle path on the other side of the roadway. But then, when you are on the force you must do your duty.

One afternoon as Skipper was standing post like this he caught a new note that rose above the hum of the park traffic. It was the quick, nervous beat of hoofs which rang sharply on the hard macadam. There were screams, too. It was a runaway. Skipper knew this even before he saw the bell-like nostrils, the straining eyes, and the foam-flecked lips of the horse, or the scared man in the carriage behind. It was a case of broken rein.

How the sight made Skipper's blood tingle! Wouldn't he just like to show that crazy roan what real running was! But what was Reddy going to do? He felt him gather up the reins. He felt his knees tighten. What! Yes, it must be so. Reddy was actually going to try a brush with the runaway. What fun!

Skipper pranced out into the roadway and gathered himself for the sport. Before he could get into full swing, however, the roan had shot past with a snort of challenge which could not be misunderstood.

"Oho! You will, eh?" thought Skipper. "Well now, we'll see about that."

Ah, a free rein! That is—almost free. And a touch of the spurs! No need for that, Reddy. How the carriages scatter!

Skipper caught hasty glimpses of smart hackneys drawn up trembling by the roadside, of women who tumbled from bicycles into the bushes, and of men who ran and shouted and waved their hats.

"Just as though that little roan wasn't scared enough already," thought Skipper.

But she did run well; Skipper had to admit that. She had a lead of fifty yards before he could strike his best gait. Then for a few moments he could not seem to gain an inch. But the mare was blowing herself and Skipper was taking it coolly. He was putting the pent-up energy of weeks into his strides. Once he saw he was overhauling her he steadied to the work.

Just as Skipper was about to forge ahead, Reddy did a queer thing. With his right hand he grabbed the roan with a nose-pinch grip, and with the left he pulled in on the reins. It was a great disappointment to Skipper, for he had counted on showing the roan his heels. Skipper knew, after two or three experiences of this kind, that this was the usual thing.

Those were glorious runs, though. Skipper wished they would come more often. Sometimes there would be two and even three in a day. Then a fortnight or so would pass without a single runaway on Skipper's beat. But duty is duty.

During the early morning hours, when there were few people in the park, Skipper's education progressed. He learned to pace around in a circle, lifting each forefoot with a sway of the body and a pawing movement which was quite rhythmical. He learned to box with his nose. He learned to walk sedately behind Reddy and to pick up a glove, dropped apparently by accident. There was always a sugar-plum or a sweet cracker in the

[11]

glove, which he got when Reddy stopped and Skipper, poking his nose over his shoulder, let the glove fall into his hands.

As he became more accomplished he noticed that "Reddy" took more pains with his toilet. Every morning Skipper's coat was curried and brushed and rubbed with chamois until it shone almost as if it had been varnished. His fetlocks were carefully trimmed, a ribbon braided into his forelock, and his hoofs polished as brightly as Reddy's boots. Then there were apples and carrots and other delicacies which Reddy brought him.

So it happened that one morning Skipper heard the Sergeant tell Reddy that he had been detailed for the Horse Show squad. Reddy had saluted and said nothing at the time, but when they were once out on post he told Skipper all about it.

"Sure an' it's app'arin' before all the

SKIPPER

swells in town you'll be, me b'y. Phat
do ye think of that, eh ? An' mebbe ye'll
be gettin' a blue ribbon, Skipper, me lad ;
an' mebbe Mr. Patrick Martin will have
a roundsman's berth an' chevrons on his
sleeves afore the year's out."

The Horse Show was all that Reddy
had promised, and more. The light almost dazzled Skipper. The sounds and
the smells confused him. But he felt
Reddy on his back, heard him chirrup
softly, and soon felt at ease on the tan-
bark.

Then there was a great crash of noise
and Skipper, with some fifty of his friends
on the force, began to move around the
circle. First it was fours abreast, then
by twos, and then a rush to troop front,
when, in a long line, they swept around
as if they had been harnessed to a beam
by traces of equal length.

After some more evolutions a half-dozen were picked out and put through their paces. Skipper was one of these. Then three of the six were sent to join the rest of the squad. Only Skipper and two others remained in the centre of the ring. Men in queer clothes, wearing tall black hats, showing much white shirt-front and carrying long whips, came and looked them over carefully.

Skipper showed these men how he could waltz in time to the music, and the people who banked the circle as far up as Skipper could see shouted and clapped their hands until it seemed as if a thunderstorm had broken loose. At last one of the men in tall hats tied a blue ribbon on Skipper's bridle.

When Reddy got him into the stable, he fed him four big red apples, one after the other. Next day Skipper knew that he was a famous horse. Reddy showed him their pictures in the paper.

SKIPPER

For a whole year Skipper was the pride of the force. He was shown to visitors at the stables. He was patted on the nose by the Mayor. The Chief, who was a bigger man than the Mayor, came up especially to look at him. In the park Skipper did his tricks every day for ladies in fine dress who exclaimed, "How perfectly wonderful!" as well as for pretty nurse-maids who giggled and said, "Now did you ever see the likes o' that, Norah?"

And then came the spavin. Ah, but that was the beginning of the end! Were you ever spavined? If so, you know all about it. If you haven't, there's no use trying to tell you. Rheumatism? Well, that may be bad; but a spavin is worse.

For three weeks Reddy rubbed the lump on the hock with stuff from a brown bottle, and hid it from the inspector. Then, one black morning, the lump was discovered. That day Skipper did not go out on post. Reddy came into the stall, put his arm around his neck and said "Good-by" in a voice that Skipper had never heard him use before. Something had made it thick and husky. Very sadly Skipper saw him saddle one of the new-comers and go out for duty.

Before Reddy came back Skipper was led away. He was taken to a big build-ing where there were horses of every kind —except the right kind. Each one had his own peculiar "out," although you couldn't always tell what it was at first glance.

But Skipper did not stay here long. He was led into a big ring before a lot of men. A man on a box shouted out a number, and began to talk very fast. Skipper gathered that he was talking about him. Skipper learned that he was still only six years old, and that he had been owned as a saddle-horse by a lady who was about to sail for Europe and was closing out her stable. This was news to Skipper. He wished Reddy could hear it.

The man talked very nicely about Skipper. He said he was kind, gentle, sound in wind and limb, and was not only trained to the saddle but would work either single or double. The man wanted to know how much the gentlemen were willing to pay for a bay gelding of this description.

Someone on the outer edge of the crowd said, "Ten dollars."

At this the man on the box grew quite indignant. He asked if the other man wouldn't like a silver-mounted harness and a lap-robe thrown in.

"Fifteen," said another man.

Somebody else said "Twenty," another man said, "Twenty-five," and still another, "Thirty." Then there was a hitch. The man on the box began to talk very fast indeed:

"Thutty-thutty-thutty-thutty — do I hear the five? Thutty-thutty-thutty-thutty—will you make it five?"

"Thirty-five," said a red-faced man who had pushed his way to the front and was looking Skipper over sharply.

The man on the box said "Thutty-five" a good many times and asked if he "heard forty." Evidently he did not, for he stopped and said very slowly and distinctly, looking expectantly around: "Are you all done? Thirty-five—once. Thirty-five—twice. Third—and last call —sold, for thirty-five dollars!"

When Skipper heard this he hung his head. When you have been a $250 blue-ribboner and the pride of the force it is sad to be "knocked down" for thirty-five.

The next year of Skipper's life was a dark one. We will not linger over it. The red-faced man who led him away was a grocer. He put Skipper in the shafts of a heavy wagon very early every morning and drove him a long ways through the city to a big down-town market where men in long frocks shouted and handled boxes and barrels. When the wagon was heavily loaded the red-faced man drove him back to the store. Then a tow-haired boy, who jerked viciously on the lines and was fond of using the whip, drove him recklessly about the streets and avenues.

But one day the tow-haired boy pulled the near rein too hard while rounding a corner and a wheel was smashed against a lamp-post. The tow-haired boy was sent head first into an ash-barrel, and Skipper, rather startled at the occurrence, took a little run down the avenue, strewing the pavement with eggs, sugar, canned corn, celery, and other assorted groceries.

Perhaps this was why the grocer sold him. Skipper pulled a cart through the flat-house district for a while after that. On the seat of the cart sat a leather-lunged man who roared: "A-a-a-a-puls! Nice a-a-a-a-puls! A who-o-ole lot fer a quarter!"

Skipper felt this disgrace keenly. Even the cab-horses, on whom he used to look with disdain, eyed him scornfully. Skipper stood it as long as possible and then one day, while the apple fakir was standing on the back step of the cart shouting things at a woman who was leaning half way out of a fourth-story window, he bolted. He distributed that load of apples over four blocks, much to the profit of the street children, and he wrecked the wagon on a hydrant. For this the fakir beat him with a piece of the wreckage until a blue-coated officer threatened to arrest him. Next day Skipper was sold again.

SKIPPER

Skipper looked over his new owner without joy. The man was evil of face. His long whiskers and hair were unkempt and sun-bleached, like the tip end of a pastured cow's tail. His clothes were greasy. His voice was like the grunt of a pig. Skipper wondered to what use this man would put him. He feared the worst.

Far up through the city the man took him and out on a broad avenue where there were many open spaces, most of them fenced in by huge bill-boards. Behind one of these sign-plastered barriers Skipper found his new home. The bottom of the lot was more than twenty feet below the street-level. In the centre of a waste of rocks, ash-heaps, and dead weeds tottered a group of shanties, strangely made of odds and ends. The walls were partly of mud-chinked rocks and partly of wood. The roofs were patched with strips of rusty tin held in place by stones.

Into one of these shanties, just tall enough for Skipper to enter and no more, the horse that had been the pride of the mounted park police was driven with a kick as a greeting. Skipper noted first that there was no feed-box and no hay-rack. Then he saw, or rather felt—for the only light came through cracks in the walls—that there was no floor. His nostrils told him that the drainage was bad. Skipper sighed as he thought of the clean, sweet straw which Reddy used to change in his stall every night.

But when you have a lump on your leg —a lump that throbs, throbs, throbs with pain, whether you stand still or lie down —you do not think much on other things.

Supper was late in coming to Skipper that night. He was almost starved when it was served. And such a supper!

SKIPPER

What do you think? Hay? Yes, but
marsh hay; the dry, tasteless stuff they
use for bedding in cheap stables. A ton
of it wouldn't make a pound of good flesh.
Oats? Not a sign of an oat! But with
the hay there were a few potato-peelings.
Skipper nosed them out and nibbled the
marsh hay. The rest he pawed back
under him, for the whole had been thrown
at his feet. Then he dropped on the ill-
smelling ground and went to sleep to
dream that he had been turned into a
forty-acre field of clover, while a dozen
brass bands played a waltz and multi-
tudes of people looked on and cheered.

In the morning more salt hay was
thrown to him and water was brought in
a dirty pail. Then, without a stroke of
brush or curry-comb he was led out.
When he saw the wagon to which he was
to be hitched Skipper hung his head. He
had reached the bottom. It was un-

painted and rickety as to body and frame, the wheels were unmated and dished, while the shafts were spliced and wound with wire.

But worst of all was the string of bells suspended from two uprights above the seat. When Skipper saw these he knew he had fallen low indeed. He had become the horse of a wandering junkman. The next step in his career, as he well knew, would be the glue factory and the bone-yard. Now when a horse has lived for twenty years or so, it is sad enough to face these things. But at eight years to see the glue factory close at hand is enough to make a horse wish he had never been foaled.

For many weary months Skipper pulled that crazy cart, with its hateful jangle of bells, about the city streets and suburban roads while the man with the faded hair roared through his matted beard: " Buy

For many weary months Skipper pulled that crazy cart.

SKIPPER

o-o-o-o-olt ra-a-a-a-ags! Buy o-o-o-o-
olt ra-a-a-a-ags! Olt boddles! Olt copper! Olt iron! Vaste baber!"

The lump on Skipper's hock kept growing bigger and bigger. It seemed as if
the darts of pain shot from hoof to flank
with every step. Big hollows came over
his eyes. You could see his ribs as plain-
ly as the hoops on a pork-barrel. Yet
six days in the week he went on long
trips and brought back heavy loads of
junk. On Sunday he hauled the junkman and his family about the city.

Once the junkman tried to drive Skipper into one of the Park entrances.
Then for the first time in his life Skipper
balked. The junkman pounded and used
such language as you might expect from
a junkman, but all to no use. Skipper
took the beating with lowered head, but
go through the gate he would not. So
the junkman gave it up, although he

[25]

seemed very anxious to join the line of gay carriages which were rolling in.

Soon after this there came a break in the daily routine. One morning Skipper was not led out as usual. In fact, no one came near him, and he could hear no voices in the near-by shanty. Skipper decided that he would take a day off himself. By backing against the door he readily pushed it open, for the staple was insecure.

Once at liberty, he climbed the roadway that led out of the lot. It was late in the fall, but there was still short sweet winter grass to be found along the gutters. For a while he nibbled at this hungrily. Then a queer idea came to Skipper. Perhaps the passing of a smartly groomed saddle-horse was responsible.

At any rate, Skipper left off nibbling grass. He hobbled out to the edge of the road, turned so as to face the opposite

side, and held up his head. There he
stood just as he used to stand when he
was the pride of the mounted squad. He
was on post once more.

Few people were passing, and none
seemed to notice him. Yet he was an
odd figure. His coat was shaggy and
weather-stained. It looked patched and
faded. The spavined hock caused one
hind quarter to sag somewhat, but aside
from that his pose was strictly according
to the regulations.

Skipper had been playing at standing
post for a half-hour, when a trotting
dandy who sported ankle-boots and toe-
weights, pulled up before him. He was
drawing a light, bicycle-wheeled road-
wagon in which were two men.

"Queer?" one of the men was saying.
"Can't say I see anything queer about it,
Captain. Some old plug that's got away
from a squatter; that's all I see in it."

"Well, let's have a look," said the other. He stared hard at Skipper for a moment and then, in a loud, sharp tone, said:

"'Ten-shun! Right dress!'"

Skipper pricked up his ears, raised his head, and side-stepped stiffly. The trotting dandy turned and looked curiously at him.

"Forward!" said the man in the wagon. Skipper hobbled out into the road.

"Right wheel! Halt! I thought so," said the man, as Skipper obeyed the orders. "That fellow has been on the force. He was standing post. Looks mighty familiar, too—white stockings on two forelegs, white star on forehead. Now I wonder if that can be—here, hold the reins a minute."

Going up to Skipper the man patted his nose once or twice, and then pushed his muzzle to one side. Skipper ducked

and countered. He had not forgotten his
boxing trick. The man turned his back
and began to pace down the road. Skipper followed and picked up a riding-glove
which the man dropped.

"Doyle," said the man, as he walked
back to the wagon, "two years ago that
was the finest horse on the force—took
the blue ribbon at the Garden. Alderman Martin would give $1,000 for him
as he stands. He has hunted the State
for him. You remember Martin—Reddy
Martin—who used to be on the mounted
squad! Didn't you hear? An old uncle
who made a fortune as a building con-
tractor died about a year ago and left
the whole pile to Reddy. He's got a
fine country place up in Westchester and
is in the city government. Just elected
this fall. But he isn't happy because he
can't find his old horse—and here's the
horse."

Next day an astonished junkman stood before an empty shanty which served as a stable and feasted his eyes on a fifty-dollar bank-note.

If you are ever up in Westchester County be sure to visit the stables of Alderman P. Sarsfield Martin. Ask to see that oak-panelled box-stall with the stained-glass windows and the porcelain feed-box. You will notice a polished brass name-plate on the door bearing this inscription:

SKIPPER.

You may meet the Alderman himself, wearing an English-made riding-suit, loping comfortably along on a sleek bay gelding with two white forelegs and a white star on his forehead. Yes, high-priced veterinaries can cure spavin—Alderman Martin says so.

CALICO

WHO TRAVELLED WITH A
ROUND TOP

CALICO

WHO TRAVELLED WITH A
ROUND TOP

SOMETHING there was about Calico's markings which stuck in one's
mind, as does a haunting memory, intan-
gible but unforgotten. Surely the pattern was obtrusive enough to halt attention; yet its vagaries were so unexpected,
so surprising that, even as you looked,
you might hesitate at declaring whether
it was his withers or his flanks which
were carrot-red and if he had four white
stockings or only three. It was safer
simply to say that he was white where he
was not red and red where he was not
white. Moreover, his was a vivid coat.

Altogether Calico was a horse to be re-marked and to be remembered. Yet—and again yet—Calico was not wholly to blame for his many faults. Farm breed-ing, which was more or less responsible for his bizarre appearance, should also bear the burden of his failings. As a colt he had been the marvel of the county, from Orono to Hermon Centre. He had been petted, teased, humored, exhibited, coddled, fooled with—everything save properly trained and broken.

So he grew up a trace shirker and a halter-puller, with disposition, tempera-ment, and general behavior as uneven as his coloring.

"The most good-fer-nothin' animal I ever wasted grain on!" declared Uncle Enoch.

For the better part of four unproduc-tive years had the life of Calico run to commonplaces. Then, early one June

[34]

morning, came an hour big with events.
Being the nigh horse in Uncle Enoch's
pair, Calico caught first glimpse of the
weird procession which met them as they
turned into the Bangor road at Sher-
burne's Corners.

Now it was Calico's habit to be on the
watch for unusual sights, and when he
saw them to stick his ears forward, throw
his head up, snort nervously and crowd
against the pole. Generally he got one
leg over a trace. There was a white
bowlder at the top of Poorhouse Hill
which Calico never passed without going
through some of these manœuvres.

"Hi-i-ish there! So-o-o! Dern yer
crazy-quilt hide. Body'd think yer never
see that stun afore in yer life. Gee-long
a-a-ap!" Uncle Enoch would growl, ac-
centing his words by jerking the lines.

A scarecrow in the middle of a corn-
field, an auction bill tacked to a stump,

an old hat stuffing a vacant pane and pro-
claiming the shiftlessness of the Aroostook
Billingses, would serve when nothing else
offered excuse for skittishness. Even
sober Old Jeff, the off horse, sometimes
caught the infection for a moment. He
would prick up his ears and look inquiringly at the suspected object, but so soon
as he saw what it was down went his
head sheepishly, as if he was ashamed of
having again been tricked.

This morning, however, it was no false
alarm. When Old Jeff was roused out
of his accustomed jog by Calico's nervous
snorts he looked up to see such a spectacle as he had never beheld in all his
goings and comings up and down the
Bangor road. Looming out of the mist
was a six-horse team hitched to the most
foreign-looking rig one could well imagine. It had something of the look of a
preposterous hay-cart, with the ends of

blue-painted poles sticking out in front
and trailing behind. Following this was
a great, white-swathed wheeled box drawn
by four horses. It was certainly a curious affair, whatever it was, but neither
Calico nor Old Jeff gave it much heed,
nor did they waste a glance on the distant tail of the procession, for behind the
wheeled box was a thing which held their
gaze.

In the gray four o'clock light it seemed
like an enormous cow that rolled menacingly forward ; not as a cow walks, however, but with a swaying, heaving motion
like nothing commonly seen on a Maine
highway. Instinctively both horses thrust
their muzzles toward the thing and sniffed.
Without doubt Old Jeff was frightened.
Perhaps not for nine generations had any
of his ancestors caught a whiff of that
peculiarly terrifying scent of which every
horse inherits knowledge and dread.

As for Calico, he had no need of such spur as inherited terror. He had fearsomeness enough of his own to send him rearing and pawing the air until the whiffle-trees rapped his knees. Old Jeff did not rear. He stared and snorted and trembled. When he felt his mate spring forward in the traces he went with him, ready to do anything in order to get away from that heaving, swaying thing which was coming toward them.

" Whoa, ye pesky fools! Whoa, dod rot ye!" Uncle Enoch, wakened from the half doze which he had been taking on the wagon-seat, now began to saw on the lines. His shouts seemed to have aroused the heaving thing, for it answered with a horrid, soul-chilling noise.

By this time Calico was leaping frantically, snorting at every jump and forcing Old Jeff to keep pace. They were at the top of a long grade and down the slope the loaded wagon rattled easily behind them. Uncle Enoch did his best. With feet well braced he tugged at the lines and shouted, all to no purpose. Never before had Calico and Old Jeff met a circus on the move. Neither had they previously come into such close quarters with an elephant. One does not expect such things on the Bangor road. At least they did not. They proposed to get away from such terrors in the shortest possible time.

Now the public ways of Maine are seldom macadamized. In places they are laid out straight across and over the granite back-bone of the continent. The Bangor road is thus constructed in spots. This slope was one of the spots where the bare ledge, with here and there six-inch shelves and eroded gullies, offered a somewhat uneven surface to the wheels. A well built Studebaker will stand a lot of this kind of banging, but it is not wholly indestructible. So it happened that half-way down the hill the left hind axle snapped at the hub. Thereupon some two hundred dozen ears of early green-corn were strewn along the flinty face of the highway, while Uncle Enoch was hurled, seat and all, accompanied by four dozen eggs and ten pounds of Aunt Henrietta's best butter, into the ditch.

When the circus caravan overtook him Uncle Enoch had captured the runaways and was leading them back to where the wrecked wagon lay by the roadside. More or less butter was mixed with the sandy chin whiskers and an inartistic yellow smooch down the front of his coat showed that the eggs had followed him.

"Rather lively pair of yours; eh, mister?" commented a red-faced man who dropped off the pole-wagon.

" Yes, ruther lively," assented Uncle Enoch, " 'Specially when ye don't want 'em to be. The off one's stiddy enough. It's this cantankerous skewbald that started the tantrum. Whoa now, blame ye!" Calico's nose was in the air again and he was snorting excitedly.

" Lemme hold him 'till old Ajax goes by," said the circus man.

"'Thank ye. I'll swap him off fust chance I git, ef I don't fetch back nuthin' but a boneyard skate," declared Uncle Enoch.

As Ajax lumbered by, the circus man eyed with interest the dancing Calico. He noted with approval the coat of fantastic design, the springy knees and the fine tail that rippled its white length almost to Calico's heels.

" I'll do better'n that by you, mister," said he. " I've got a fourteen-hundred pound Vermont Morgan, sound as a dollar, only eight years old and ain't afraid o' nothin'. I'll swap him even for your skewbald."

"Like to see him," said Uncle Enoch. "If he's half what ye say it's a trade."

"Here he comes on the band-wagon team;" then, to the driver: "Hey, Bill, pull up!"

In less than half an hour from the time Calico had bolted at sight of the circus cavalcade he was part and parcel of it, and helping to pull one of those mysterious sheeted wagons along in the wake of the terrifying Ajax.

"The old party don't give you a very good send off," said the boss hostler reflectively to Calico, "but I reckon you'll get used to Ajax and the music-chariot before the season's over. Leastways, you're bound to be an ornament to the grand entry."

Calico's life with the Grand Occidental began abruptly and vigorously. The

driver of the band-wagon knew his business. Even when half asleep he could
see loose traces. After Calico had heard
the long lash whistle about his ears a few
times he concluded that it was best to do
his share of the pulling.

And what pulling it was! There were
six horses of them, Calico being one of
the swings, but on an uphill grade that
old chariot was the most reluctant thing
he had ever known. Uncle Enoch's
stone-boat, which Calico had once held
to be merely a heart-breaking instrument
of torture, seemed light in retrospect.
Often did he look reproachfully at the
monstrous combination of gilded wood
and iron. Why need band-wagons be
made so exasperatingly heavy? The
atrociously carved Pans on the corners,
with their scarred faces and broken pipes,
were cumbersome enough to make a load
for one pair of horses, all by themselves.

Calico would think of them as he was straining up a long hill. He could almost feel them pulling back on the traces in a sort of wooden stubbornness. And when the team rattled the old chariot down a rough grade how he hoped that two or three of the figures might be jolted off. But in the morning, when the show lot was reached and the travelling wraps taken off the wagons, there he would see the heavy shouldered Pans all in their places as hideous and as permanent as ever.

It was a hard and bitter lesson which Calico learned, this matter of keeping one's tugs tight. Uncle Enoch had spared the whip, but in the heart of Broncho Bill, who drove the band-wagon, there was no leniency. Ready and strong was his whip hand, and he knew how to make the blood follow the lash. No effort did he waste on fat-padded flanks

when he was in earnest. He cut at the
ears, where the skin is tender. He could
touch up the leaders as easily as he could
the wheel-horses, and when he aimed at
the swings he never missed fire.

Travelling with a round top Calico
found to be no sinecure. The Grand
Occidental, being a wagon show, moved
wholly by road. The shortest jump was
fifteen miles, but often they did thirty between midnight and morning; and thirty
miles over country highways make no
short jaunt when you have a five-ton
chariot behind you. The jump, however,
was only the beginning of the day's work.
No sooner had you finished breakfast than
you were hooked in for the street parade,
meaning from two to four miles more.

You had a few hours for rest after that
before the grand entry. Ah, that grand
entry! That was something to live for.
No matter how bad the roads or how

hard the hills had been Calico forgot it
all during those ten delightful minutes
when, with his heart beating time to the
rat-tat-tat of the snare drum, he swung
prancingly around the yellow arena.

It all began in the dressing-tent with
a period of confusion in which horses
were crowded together as thick as they
could stand, while the riders dressed and
mounted in frantic haste, for to be late
meant to be fined. At last the ring-master clapped his hands as sign that all was
in readiness. There was a momentary
hush. Then a bugle sounded, the flaps
were thrown back and to the crashing accompaniment of the band, the seemingly
chaotic mass unfolded into a double line
as the horses broke into a sharp gallop
around the freshly dug ring.

The first time Calico did the grand entry he felt as though he had been sucked
into a whirlpool and was being carried

around by some irresistible force. So
dazed was he by the music, by the hum
of human voices and by the unfamiliar
sights, that he forgot to rear and kick.
He could only prance and snort. He
went forward because the rider of the
outside horse dragged him along by the
bridle rein. Around and around he circled until he lost all sense of direction,
and when he was finally shunted out
through the dressing-tent flaps he was so
dizzy he could scarcely stand.

For a horse accustomed to shy at his
own shadow this was heroic treatment.
But it was successful. In a month you
could not have startled Calico with a
pound of dynamite. He would placidly
munch his oats within three feet of the
spot where a stake-gang swung the heavy
sledges in staccato time. He cared no
more for flapping canvas than for the
wagging of a mule's ears. As for noises,

when one has associated with a steam
calliope one ceases to mind anything in
that line. Old Ajax, it was true, remained a terror to Calico for weeks, but
in the end the horse lost much of his
dread for the ancient pachyderm, although he never felt wholly comfortable
while those wicked little eyes were turned
in his direction. Hereditary instincts,
you know, die hard.

During those four months in which the
Grand Occidental flitted over the New
England circuit from Kenduskeag, Me.,
to Bennington, Vt., there came upon
Calico knowledge of many things. The
farm-horse to whom Bangor's market-
square had been full of strange sights became, in comparison with his former self,
most sophisticated. He feared no noise
save that sinister whistle made by Broncho Bill's long lash. The roaring sputter
of gasoline flares was no more to him

than the sound of a running brook. He had learned that it was safe to kick a mere canvasman when you felt like doing so, but that a real artist, such as a tumbler or a trapeze man, was to be respected, and that the person of the ringmaster was most sacred. Also he acquired the knack of sleeping at odd times, whenever opportunity offered and under any conditions.

When he had grown thus wise, and when he had ceased to stumble over guy-ropes and tent-stakes, Calico received promotion. He was put in as outside horse of the leading pair in the grand entry. He was decorated with a white-braided cord bridle with silk rosettes and he wore between his ears a feather pompon. All this was very fine and grand, but there was so little of it.

After it was all over, when the crowds had gone, the top lowered and the stakes pulled, he was hitched to the leaden-wheeled band-wagon to strain and tug at the traces all through the last weary half of the night. But when fame has started your way, be you horse or man, you cannot escape. Just before the season closed Calico was put on the sawdust. This was the way of it.

A ninety-foot top, you know, carries neither extra people nor spare horses. The performers must double up their acts. No one is exempt save the autocratic high-bar folk, who own their own apparatus and dictate contracts. So with the horses. The teams that pull the pole-wagon, the chariots and the other wheeled things which a circus needs, must also figure in the grand entry and in the hippodrome races. Even the ring-horses have their share of road-work in a wagon show.

To the dappled grays used by Mlle. Zaretti, who was a top-liner on the bills,

fell the lot of pulling the ticket-wagon,
this being the lightest work. It was
Mlle. Zaretti's habit to ride one at the
afternoon show, the other in the evening.
So when the nigh gray developed a shoulder gall on the day that the off one went
lame there arose an emergency. Also
there ensued trouble for the driver of
the ticket-wagon. First he was tongue
lashed by Mademoiselle, then he was
fined a week's pay and threatened with
discharge by the manager. But when
the increasing wrath of the Champion
Lady Equestrienne of America led her to
demand his instant and painful annihila-
tion the worm turned. The driver pro-
fanely declared that he knew his business.
He had travelled with Yank Robinson,
he had, and no female hair-grabber under
canvas should call him down more than
once in the same day. There was more
of this, added merely for emphasis. Mlle.

Zaretti saw the point. She had gone too far. Whereupon she discreetly turned on her high French heels and meekly asked the boss hostler for the most promising animal he had. The boss picked out Calico.

No sooner was the top up that day than Calico's training began. Well it was that he had learned obedience, for this was to be his one great opportunity. Many a time had Calico circled around the banked ring's outer circumference, but never had he been within it. Neither had he worn before a broad pad. By dint of leading and coaxing he was made to understand that his part of the act was to canter around the ring with Mlle. Zaretti on his back, where she was to be allowed to go through as many motions as she pleased.

For a green horse Calico conducted himself with much credit. He did not stumble. He did not shy at the ring-master's whip. He did not try to dodge the banners or the hoops after he found how harmless they were.

" Well, if I cut my act perhaps I can manage, but if I break my neck I hope you'll murder that fool driver," was Mlle. Zaretti's verdict and petition when the lesson ended.

Mlle. Zaretti's gyrations that afternoon and evening were somewhat tame when you consider the manner in which she was billed. Calico did his part with only a few excusable blunders, and she was so pleased that he got the apples and sugar-plums which usually rewarded the grays.

The galled shoulder healed, but the lame leg developed into an incurably stiff joint. Three nights later Calico, to his great joy, left the band-chariot team for-ever, to find himself on the light ticket-wagon and regularly entered as a ring horse. Nor was this all. When the season closed Mlle. Zaretti bought Calico at an exorbitant price. He was shipped to a strange place, where they put him in a box-stall, fed him with generous regularity and asked him to do absolutely nothing at all.

It was a month before Calico saw his mistress again. He had been taken into a great barn-like structure which had many sky-lights and windows. Here was an ideal ring, smooth and springy, with no hidden rocks or soft spots such as one sometimes finds when on the road. Mlle. Zaretti no longer wore her spangled pink dress. Instead she appeared in serviceable knickerbockers and wore wooden-soled slippers on her feet. In the middle of the ring a man who was turning himself into a human pin-wheel stopped long enough to shout : "Hello, Kate ; signed yet?"

"You bet," said Mlle. Zaretti. "Next spring I go out by rail with a three top-

per. I'm going to do the real bareback
act, too. No more broad pads and wagon
shows for Katie. Hey, Jim, rig up your
Stokes' mechanic."

Jim, a stout man who wore his sus-
penders outside a blue sweater and talked
huskily, arranged a swinging derrick-arm,
the purpose of which, it developed, was
to keep Mlle. Zaretti off the ground
whenever she missed her footing on Calico's back. There was a broad leather
belt around her waist and to this was
fastened a rope. Very often was this
needed during those first three weeks of
practice, for, true to her word, Mlle. Zaretti no longer strapped on Calico's back
the broad pad to which he had been accustomed. At first the wooden-soles
hurt and made him flinch, but in time the
skin became toughened and he minded
them not at all, although Mlle. Zaretti
was no featherweight.

Long before the snow was gone Mlle. Zaretti had discarded the derrick-arm. Urging Calico to his best speed she would grasp the cinch handles and with one light bound land on his well-resined back. Then, as he circled around in an even, rythmical lope, she would jump the banners and dive through the hoops. It was more or less fun for Calico, but it all seemed so utterly useless. There were no crowds to see and applaud. He missed the music and the cheering.

At last there came a change. Calico and his mistress took a journey. They arrived in the biggest city Calico had ever seen, and one afternoon, to the accompaniment of such a crash of music and such a chorus of " HI! HI! HI's!" as he had never before heard, they burst into a great arena where were not only one ring but three, and about them, tier on tier as far up as one could see, the eager faces and gay clothes of a vast multitude of spectators. Calico, as you will guess, had become a factor in " The Grandest Aggregation."

If Calico had longed for music and applause his wishes were surely answered, for, although Mlle. Zaretti had jumped from a wagon-show to a three-ring combination that began its season with an indoor March opening, she was still a top-liner. That is, she had a feature act.

Thus it was that just as the Japanese jugglers finished tossing each other on their toes in the upper ring and while the property helpers were making ready the lower one for the elephants, in the centre ring Mlle. Zaretti and Calico alone held the attention of great audiences.

" Mem-zelle Zar-ret-ti! Champ-i-on la-dy bare-back ri-der of the wor-r-r-r-ld, on her beaut-i-ful Ar-a-bian steed!"

HORSES NINE

That was the manner in which the megaphone announcer heralded their appearance. Then followed a rattle of drums and a tooting of horns, ending in one tremendous bang as Calico, lifting his feet so high and so daintily you might have thought he was stepping over a row of china vases, and bowing his head so low that his neck arched almost double, came mincing into the arena. In his mouth he champed solid silver bits, and his polished hoofs were rimmed with nickel-plated shoes. The heavy bridle reins were covered with the finest white kid, as was the surcingle which completed his trappings.

Rather stout had Calico become in these halcyon days. His back and flanks were like the surface of a well-upholstered sofa. His coat of motley told its own story of daily rubbings and good feeding. The white was dazzlingly white and the

CALICO

carrot-red patches glowed like the inside of a well-burnished copper kettle. So shiny was he that you could see reflected on his sides the black, gold-spangled tights and fluffy black skirts worn by Mlle. Zaretti, who poised on his back as lightly as if she had been an ostrich-plume dropped on a snow-bank and who smilingly kissed her finger-tips to the craning-necked tiers of spectators with charming indiscrimination and admirable impartiality.

You may imagine that this picture was not without its effect. Never did it fail to draw forth a mighty volume of " Ohs !" and " Ah-h-h-hs !" especially at the after-noon performances, when the youngsters were out in force. And how Calico did relish this hum of admiration ! Perhaps Mlle. Zaretti thought some of it was meant for her. No such idea had Calico.

You could see this by the way in which

he tossed his head and pawed haughtily as he waited for the band to strike up his music. Oh, yes, *his* music. You must know that by this time the horse that had once pulled the stone-boat on Uncle Enoch's farm, and had later learned the hard lesson of obedience under Broncho Bill's lash had now become an equine personage. He had his grooms and his box-stall. He had whims which must be humored. One of these had to do with the music which played him through his act. He had discovered that the Blue Danube waltz was exactly to his liking, and to no other tune would he consent to do his best. Sulking was one of his new accomplishments.

As for Mlle. Zaretti, she affected no such frills, but she was ever ready to defend those of her horse. A hard-working, frugal, ambitious young person was Mlle. Zaretti, whose few extravagances were mostly on Calico's account. For him she demanded the Blue Danube waltz in the face of the band-master's grumblings.

When the Grandest Aggregation finally took the road the satisfaction of Calico was complete. He was under canvas once more. No band-wagon work wearied his nights. He even enjoyed the street parade. In the evening, when his act was over, he left the tents, glowing huge and brilliant against the night, and jogged quietly off to his padded car-stall, where were to be had a full two hours' rest before No. 2 train pulled out.

In the gray of the morning he would wake to contentedly look out through his grated window at the flying landscape, remembering with a sigh of satisfaction that no longer was he routed out at cock-crow to be driven afield. Later he could see the curious crowds in the railroad yards as the long lines of cars were

shunted back and forth. As he lazily
munched his breakfast oats he watched
the draught horses patiently drag the
huge chariots across the tracks and off to
the show lot where *he* was not due for
hours.

A life of mild exertion, enjoyable excitement, changing scenes, and consider-
ate treatment was his. No wonder the
fat stuck to Calico's ribs. No wonder his
eyes beamed contentment. Such are the
sweets of high achievement.

It was to sell early July peas that Uncle Enoch again took the Bangor road
one day about three years after his mem-
orable meeting with the Grand Occidental. On his way across the city to No-
rumbega Market he found his way blocked
by a line of waiting people. From an ur-
chin-tossed handbill, Uncle Enoch learned
that the Grandest Aggregation was in

town and that "the Unparalleled Street
Pageant" was about due.   So he waited.

With grim enjoyment Uncle Enoch
watched the brilliant spectacle impassive-
ly. Old Jeff merely pricked up his ears in
curious interest as the procession moved
along in its dazzling course.

"Zaretti, Bareback Queen of the
World!   On her Famous Arabian Steed
Abdullah! Presented to her by the Shah
of Persia!"

Thus read Uncle Enoch as he followed
the printed order of parade with toil-
grimed forefinger.

For a moment Uncle Enoch's gaze was
held by the Bareback Queen, who looked
languidly into space over the top of the
tiger cage.   Then he stared hard at the
"far-famed Arabian steed," gift of the
impulsive Shah.   Said steed was capari-
soned in a gorgeous saddle-blanket hung
with silver fringe.   A silver-mounted

martingale dangled between his knees. Holding the silk-tasselled bridle rein, and walking in respectful attendance, was a groom in tight-fitting riding breeches and a cockaded hat which rested mainly on his ears. The horse was of white, mottled with carrot-red in such striking pattern that, having once seen it, one could hardly forget.

"Gee whilikins!" said Uncle Enoch softly to himself, as if fearful of betraying some newly discovered secret.

But Old Jeff was moved to no such reticence. Lifting his head over the shoulders of the crowd he pointed his ears and gave vent to a quick, glad whinny of recognition. The "far-famed Arabian," turning so sharply that the unwary groom was knocked sprawling, looked hard at the humble farm-horse, and then, with an answering high-pitched neigh, dashed through the quickly scattering spectators.

CALICO

It was a moment of surprises. The Bareback Queen of the World was startled out of her day-dream to find her "Arabian steed" rubbing noses with a ragged-coated horse hitched to a battered farm-wagon, in which sat a chin-whiskered old fellow who grinned expansively and slyly winked at her over the horses' heads.

"It's all right, ma'am, I won't let on," he said.

Before she could reply, the groom, who had rescued his cockaded hat and his presence of mind, rushed in and dragged the far-famed steed back into the line of procession.

"Wall, I swən to man, ef Old Jeff didn't know that air Calicker afore I did," declared Uncle Enoch, as he described the affair to Aunt Henrietta; "an' me that raised him from a colt. I do swan to man!"

HORSES NINE

Mlle. Zaretti did not "swan to man," whatever that may be, but to this day she marvels concerning the one and only occasion when her trusted Calico disturbed the progress of the Grandest Aggregation's unparalleled street pageant.

OLD SILVER

A STORY OF THE GRAY
HORSE TRUCK

OLD SILVER

A STORY OF THE GRAY HORSE TRUCK

DOWN in the heart of the skyscraper district, keeping watch and ward over those presumptuous, man-made cliffs around which commerce heaps its Fundy tides, you will find, unhandsomely housed on a side street, a hook and ladder company, known unofficially and intimately throughout the department as the Gray Horse Truck.

Much like a big family is a fire company. It has seasons of good fortune, when there are neither sick leaves nor hospital cases to report ; and it has periods of misfortune, when trouble and disaster stalk abruptly through the ranks. Gray Horse Truck company is no exception. Calm prosperity it has enjoyed, and of swift, unexpected tragedy it has had full measure. Yet its longest mourning and most sincere, was when it lost Old Silver.

Although some of the men of Gray Horse Truck had seen more than ten years' continuous service in the house, not one could remember a time when Old Silver had not been on the nigh side of the poles. Mikes and Petes and Jims there had been without number. Some were good and some were bad, some had lasted years and some only months, some had been kind and some ugly, some stupid and some clever ; but there had been but one Silver, who had combined all their good traits as well as many of their bad ones.

Horses and men, Silver had seen them come and go. He had seen probationers

rise step by step to battalion and dep-
uty chiefs, win shields and promotion or
meet the sudden fate that is their lot.
All that time Silver's name-board had
swung over his old stall, and when the
truck went out Silver was to be found
in his old place on the left of the poles.
Driver succeeded driver, but one and all
they found Silver first under the harness
when a station hit, first to jump forward
when the big doors rolled back, and always as ready to do his bit on a long
run as he was to demand his four quarts
when feeding-time came.

Before the days of the Training Stable,
where now they try out new material,
Silver came into the service. That excellent institution, therefore, cannot claim
the credit of his selection. Perhaps he
was chosen by some shrewd old captain,
who knew a fire-horse when he saw one,
even in the raw ; perhaps it was only a

happy chance which put him in the business. At any rate, his training was the
work of a master hand.

Silver was not one of the fretting kind,
so at the age of fifteen he was apple-
round, his legs were straight and springy,
and his eyes as full and bright as those of
a school-boy at a circus. The dapples on
his gray flanks were as distinct as the under markings on old velours, while his tail
had the crisp whiteness of a polished steel
bit on a frosty morning. Unless you had
seen how shallow were his molar cups or
noted the length of his bridle teeth, would
you have guessed him not more than six.

As for the education of Silver, its scope
and completeness, no outsider would have
given credence to the half of it. When
Lannigan had driven the truck for three
years, and had been cronies with Silver
for nearly five, it was his habit to say,
wonderingly :

OLD SILVER

"He beats me, Old Silver does. I git onto some new wrinkle of his every day. No; 'taint no sorter use to tell his tricks; you wouldn't believe, nor would I an' I hadn't seen with me two eyes."

In the way of mischief Silver was a star performer. What other fire-horse ever mastered the intricacies of the automatic halter release? It was Silver, too, that picked from the Captain's hip-pocket a neatly folded paper and chewed the same with malicious enthusiasm. The folded paper happened to be the Company's annual report, in the writing of which the Captain had spent many weary hours.

Other things besides mischief however, had Silver learned. Chief of these was to start with the jigger. Sleeping or waking, lying or standing, the summons that stirred the men from snoring ease to tense, rapid action, never failed to find Silver alert. As the halter shank slipped

through the bit-ring that same instant
found Silver gathered for the rush through
the long narrow lane leading from his open
stall to the poles, above which, like great
couchant spiders, waited the harnesses
pendant on the hanger-rods. It was unwise to be in Silver's way when that little
brazen voice was summoning him to duty.
More than one man of Gray Horse Truck
found that out.

Once under the harness Silver was like
a carved statue until the trip-strap had
been pulled, the collar fastened and the
reins snapped in. Then he wanted to
poke the poles through the doors, so
eager was he to be off. It was no fault
of Silver's that his team could not make
a two-second hitch.

With the first strain at the traces his
impatience died out. A sixty-foot truck
starts with more or less reluctance. Besides, Silver knew that before anything

like speed could be made it was necessary either to mount the grade to Broadway or to ease the machine down to Greenwich Street. It was traces or backing-straps for all that was in you, and at the end a sharp turn which never could have been made had not the tiller-man done his part with the rear wheels.

But when once the tires caught the car-tracks Silver knew what to expect. At the turn he and his team mates could feel Lannigan gathering in the reins as though for a full stop. Next came the whistle of the whip. It swept across their flanks so quickly that it was practically one stroke for them all. At the same moment Lannigan leaned far forward and shot out his driving arm. The reins went loose, their heads went forward and, as if moving on a pivot, the three leaped as one horse. Again the reins tightened for a second, again they were loosened.

When the bits were pulled back up came
three heads, up came three pairs of shoulders and up came three pairs of forelegs;
for at the other end of the lines, gripped
vice-like in Lannigan's big fist, was swinging a good part of Lannigan's one hundred and ninety-eight pounds.

Left to themselves each horse would
have leaped at a different instant. It
was that one touch of the lash and the
succeeding swing of Lannigan's bulk
which gave them the measure, which set
the time, which made it possible for less
than four thousand pounds of horse-flesh
to jump a five-ton truck up the street at
a four-minute clip.

For Silver all other minor pleasures in
life were as nothing to the fierce joy he
knew when, with a dozen men clinging
to the hand-rails, the captain pulling the
bell-rope and Lannigan, far up above them
all, swaying on the lines, the Gray Horse

OLD SILVER

Truck swept up Broadway to a first call-box.

It was like trotting to music, if you've ever done that. Possibly you could have discovered no harmony at all in the confused roar of the apparatus as it thundered past. But to the ears of Silver there were many sounds blended into one. There were the rhythmical beat of hoofs, the low undertone of the wheels grinding the pavement, the high note of the forged steel lock-opener as it hammered the foot-board, the mellow ding-dong of the bell, the creak of the forty- and fifty-foot extensions, the rattle of the iron-shod hooks, the rat-tat-tat of the scaling ladders on the bridge and the muffled drumming of the leather helmets as they jumped in the basket.

With the increasing speed all these sounds rose in pitch until, when the team was at full-swing, they became one vi-

brant theme—thrilling, inspiring, exul-
tant—the action song of the Truck.

To enjoy such music, to know it at its
best, you must leap in the traces, feel the
swing of the poles, the pull of the whiffle-
trees, the slap of the trace-bearers; and
you must see the tangled street-traffic
clear before you as if by the wave of a
magician's wand.

Of course it all ended when, with
heaving flanks and snorting nostrils you
stopped before a building. where thin
curls of smoke escaped from upper windows. Generally you found purring beside a hydrant a shiny steamer which had
beaten the truck by perhaps a dozen sec-
onds. Then you watched your men
snatch the great ladders from the truck,
heave them up against the walls and
bring down pale-faced, staring-eyed men
and women. You saw them tear open
iron shutters, batter down doors, smash

windows and do other things to make a
path for the writhing, white-bodied, yel-
low-nosed snakes that uncoiled from the
engine and were carried wriggling in
where the flames lapped along baseboard
and floor-beams. You saw the little rip-
ples of smoke swell into huge, cream-
edged billows that tumbled out and up so
far above that you lost sight of them.

Sometimes there came dull explosions,
when smoke and flame belched out about
you. Sometimes stones and bricks and
cornices fell near you. But you were
not to flinch or stir until Lannigan, who
watched all these happenings with critical
and unwinking eyes, gave the word.

And after it was all over—when the
red and yellow flames had ceased to dance
in the empty window spaces, when only
the white steam-smoke rolled up through
the yawning roof-holes—the ladders were
re-shipped, you left the purring engines

to drown out the last hidden spark, and
you went prancing back to your House,
where the lonesome desk-man waited pa-
tiently for your return.

No loping rush was the homeward trip.
The need for haste had passed. Now
came the parade. You might toss your
head, arch your neck, and use all your
fancy steps: Lannigan didn't care. In
fact, he rather liked to have you show off
a bit. The men on the truck, smutty of
face and hands, joked across the ladders.
The strain was over. It was a time of
relaxing, for behind was duty well done.

Then came the nice accuracy of swinging a sixty-foot truck in a fifty-foot street
and of backing through a fourteen-foot
door wheels which spanned thirteen feet
from hub rim to hub rim.

After unhooking there was the rubbing
and the extra feeding of oats that always
follows a long run. How good it was to

be bedded down after this lung stretching, leg limbering work.

Such was the life which Old Silver was leading when there arrived disaster. It came in the shape of a milk leg. Perhaps it was caused by over-feeding, but more likely it resulted from much standing in stall during a fortnight when the runs had been few and short.

It behaved much as milk legs usually do. While there was no great pain the leg was unhandsome to look upon, and it gave to Old Silver a clumsiness of movement he had never known before.

Industriously did Lannigan apply such simple remedies as he had at hand. Yet the swelling increased until from pastern to hock was neither shape nor grace. Worst of all, in getting on his feet one morning, Silver barked the skin with a rap from his toe calks. Then it did look bad. Of course this had to happen just before the veterinary inspector's monthly visit.

"Old Silver, eh?" said he. "Well, I've been looking for him to give out. That's a bad leg there, a very bad leg. Send him up to the hospital in the morning, and I'll have another gray down here. It's time you had a new horse in his place."

Lannigan stepped forward to protest. It was only a milk leg. He had cured such before. He could cure this one. Besides, he couldn't spare Silver, the best horse on his team.

But the inspector often heard such pleas.

"You drivers," said he, "would keep a horse going until he dropped through the collar. To hear you talk anyone would think there wasn't another horse in the Department. What do you care so long as you get another gray?"

OLD SILVER

Very much did Lannigan care, but he found difficulty in putting his sentiments into words. Besides, of what use was it to talk to a blind fool who could say that one gray horse was as good as another. Hence Lannigan only looked sheepish and kept his tongue between his teeth until the door closed behind the inspector. Then he banged a ham-like fist into a broad palm and relieved his feelings in language both forceful and picturesque. This failed to mend matters, so Lannigan, putting an arm around the old gray's neck, told Silver all about it. Probably Silver misunderstood, for he responded by reaching over Lannigan's shoulder and chewing the big man's leather belt. Only when Lannigan fed to him six red apples and an extra quart of oats did Silver mistrust that something unusual was going to happen. Next morning, sure enough, it did happen.

Some say Lannigan wept. As to that none might be sure, for he sat facing the wall in a corner of the bunk-room. No misunderstanding could there have been about his remarks, muttered though they were. They were uncomplimentary to all veterinary inspectors in general, and most pointedly uncomplimentary to one in particular. Below they were leading Old Silver away to the hospital.

Perhaps it was that Silver's milk leg was stubborn in yielding to treatment. Perhaps the folks at the horse hospital deemed it unwise to spend time and effort on a horse of his age. At any rate, after less than a week's stay, he was cast into oblivion. They took away the leaden number medal, which for more than ten years he had worn on a strap around his neck, and they turned him over to a sales-stable as carelessly as a battalion chief would toss away a half-smoked cigar.

OLD SILVER

Now a sales-stable is a place where horse destinies are shuffled by reckless and unthinking hands. Also its doors open on the four corners of the world's crossed highways. You might go from there to find your work waiting between the shafts of a baker's cart just around the corner, or you might be sent across seas to die miserably of tsetse stings on the South African veldt.

Neither of these things happened to Silver. It occurred that his arrival at the sales-stable was coincident with a rush order from the Street Cleaning Department. So there he went. Fate, it seemed, had marked him for municipal service.

There was no delay about his initiation. Into his forehoofs they branded this shameful inscription: D. S. C. 937, on his back they flung a forty-pound single harness with a dirty piece of can-

vas as a blanket. They hooked him to
an iron dump-cart, and then, with a heavy
lashed whip, they haled him forth at 5.30
A.M. to begin the inglorious work of re-
moving refuse from the city streets.

Perhaps you think Old Silver could not
feel the disgrace, the ignominy of it all.
Could you have seen the lowered head, the
limp-hung tail, the dulled eyes and the
dispirited sag of his quarters, you would
have thought differently.

It is one thing to jump a hook and ladder truck up Broadway to the relief of
a fire-threatened block, and quite another
to plod humbly along the curb from ash-
can to ash-can. How Silver did hate
those cans. Each one should have been
for him a signal to stop. But it was not.
In consequence, he was yanked to a halt
every two minutes.

Sometimes he would crane his neck and
look mournfully around at the unsightly

[86]

leg which he had come to understand was the cause of all his misery. There would come into his great eyes a look of such pitiful melancholy that one might almost fancy tears rolling out. Then he would be roused by an exasperated driver, who jerked cruelly on the lines and used his whip as if it had been a flail.

When the cart was full Silver must drag it half across the city to the river-front, and up a steep runway from the top of which its contents were dumped into the filthy scows that waited below. At the end of each monotonous, weari-some day he jogged stiffly to the uninvit-ing stables, where he was roughly ush-ered into a dark, damp stall.

To another horse, unused to anything better, the life would not have seemed hard. Of oats and hay there were fair quantities, and there was more or less hasty grooming. But to Silver, accustomed to such little amenities as friendly pats from men, and the comradeship of his fellow-workers, it was like a bad dream. He was not even cheered by the fact that his leg, intelligently treated by the stable-boss, was growing better. What did that matter? Had he not lost his caste? Express and dray horses, the very ones that had once scurried into side streets at sound of his hoofs, now insolently crowded him to the curb. When he had been on the truck Silver had yielded the right of way to none, he had held his head high; now he dodged and waited, he wore a blind bridle, and he wished neither to see nor to be seen.

For three months Silver had pulled that hateful refuse chariot about the streets, thankful only that he traversed a section of the city new to him. Then one day he was sent out with a new driver whose route lay along familiar ways. The thing

Silver dreaded, that which he had long feared, did not happen for more than a week after the change.

It came early one morning. He had been backed up in front of a big office-building where a dozen bulky cans cumbered the sidewalk. The driver was just lifting one of them to the tail-board when, from far down the street, there reached Silver's ears a well-known sound. Nearer it swept, louder and louder it swelled. The old gray lifted his lowered head in spite of his determination not to look. The driver, too, poised the can on the cart-edge, and waited, gazing.

In a moment the noise and its cause were opposite. Old Silver hardly needed to glance before knowing the truth. It was his old company, the Gray Horse Truck. There was his old driver, there were his old team mates. In a flash there passed from Silver's mind all memory of

his humble condition, his wretched state.
Tossing his head and giving his tail a swish,
he leaped toward the apparatus, neatly
upsetting the filled ash-can over the head
and shoulders of the bewildered driver.

By a supreme effort Silver dropped into
the old lope. A dozen bounds took him
abreast the nigh horse, and, in spite of
Lannigan's shouts, there he stuck, litter-
ing the newly swept pavement most dis-
gracefully at every jump. Thus strangely
accompanied, the Gray Horse Truck thundered up Broadway for ten blocks, and
when it stopped, before a building in which
a careless watchman's lantern had set off
the automatic, Old Silver was part of the
procession.

It was Lannigan who, in the midst of
an eloquent flow of indignant abuse, made
this announcement: " Why, boys—it's—
it's our Old Silver; jiggered if it ain't ! "

Each member of the crew having expressed his astonishment in appropriate words, Lannigan tried to sum it all up by saying:

"Silver, you old sinner! So they've put you in a blanked ash-cart, have they? Well, I'll—I'll be—— "

But there speech failed him. His wits did not. There was a whispered council of war. Lannigan made a daring proposal, at which all grinned appreciatively.

"Sure, they'd never find out," said one.

"An' see, his game leg's most as good as new again," suggested another.

It was an unheard-of, audacious, and preposterous proceeding; one which the rules and regulations of the Fire Department, many and varied as they are, never anticipated. But it was adopted. Meanwhile the Captain found it necessary to inspect the interior of the building, the Lieutenant turned his back, and the thing was done.

That same evening an ill-tempered and very dirty ash-cart driver turned up at the stables with a different horse from the one he had driven out that morning, much to the mystification of himself and certain officials of the Department of Street Cleaning.

Also, there pranced back as nigh horse of the truck a big gray with one slightly swollen hind leg. By the way he held his head, by the look in his big, bright eyes, and by his fancy stepping one might have thought him glad to be where he was. And it was so. As for the rest, Lannigan will tell you in strict confidence that the best mode of disguising hoof-brands until they are effaced by new growth is to fill them with axle-grease. It cannot be detected.

Should you ever chance to see, swinging up lower Broadway, a hook-and-ladder truck drawn by three big grays jumping in perfect unison, note especially the nigh horse—that's the one on the left side looking forward. It will be Old Silver who, although now rising sixteen, seems to be good for at least another four years of active service.

BLUE BLAZES

AND THE MARRING OF HIM

BLUE BLAZES

AND THE MARRING OF HIM

THOSE who should know say that a colt may have no worse luck than to be foaled on a wet Friday. On a most amazingly wet Friday—rain above, slush below, and a March snorter roaring between—such was the natal day of Blue Blazes.

And an unhandsome colt he was. His broomstick legs seemed twice the proper length, and so thin you would hardly have believed they could ever carry him. His head, which somehow suggested the lines of a boot-jack, was set awkwardly on an ewed neck.

For this pitiful, ungainly little figure

only two in all the world had any feeling
other than contempt. One of these, of
course, was old Kate, the sorrel mare who
mothered him. She gazed at him with
sad old eyes blinded by that maternal love
common to all species, sighed with huge
content as he nuzzled for his breakfast,
and believed him to be the finest colt that
ever saw a stable. The other was Lafe,
the chore boy, who, when Farmer Perkins
had stirred the little fellow roughly with
his boot-toe as he expressed his deep dis-
satisfaction, made reparation by gently
stroking the baby colt and bringing an old
horse-blanket to wrap him in. Old Kate
understood. Lafe read gratitude in the
big, sorrowful mother eyes.

Months later, when the colt had learned
to balance himself on the spindly legs, the
old sorrel led him proudly about the pasture, showing him tufts of sweet new spring
grass, and taking him to the brook, where

were tender and juicy cowslips, finely suited to milk-teeth.

In time the slender legs thickened, the chest deepened, the barrel filled out, the head became less ungainly. As if to make up for these improvements, the colt's markings began to set. They took the shapes of a saddle - stripe, three white stockings, and an irregular white blaze covering one side of his face and patching an eye. On chest and belly the mother sorrel came out rather sharply, but on the rest of him was that peculiar blending which gives the blue roan shade, a color unpleasing to the critical eye, and one that lowers the market value.

Lafe, however, found the colt good to look upon. But Lafe himself had no heritage of beauty. He had not even grown up to his own long, thin legs. Possibly no boy ever had hair of such a homely red. Certainly few could have been found with bigger freckles. But it was his eyes which accented the plainness of his features. You know the color of a ripe gooseberry, that indefinable faint purplish tint; well, that was it.

If Lafe found no fault with Blue Blazes, the colt found no fault with Lafe. At first the colt would sniff suspiciously at him from under the shelter of the old sorrel's neck, but in time he came to regard Lafe without fear, and to suffer a hand on his flank or the chore boy's arm over his shoulder. So between them was established a gentle confidence beautiful to see.

Fortunate it would have been had Lafe been master of horse on the Perkins farm. But he was not. Firstly, there are no such officials on Michigan peach-farms; secondly, Lafe would not have filled the position had such existed. Lafe, you see, did not really belong. He was an inter-

loper, a waif who had drifted in from no-
where in particular, and who, because of
a willingness to do a man's work for no
wages at all, was allowed a place at table
and a bunk over the wagon-shed. Farmer
Perkins, more jealous of his reputation for
shrewdness than of his soul's salvation,
would point to Lafe and say, knowingly:

"He's a bad one, that boy is; look at
them eyes." And surely, if Lafe's soul-
windows mirrored the color of his mental
state, he was indeed in a bad way.

In like manner Farmer Perkins judged
old Kate's unhandsome colt.

"Look at them ears," he said, really
looking at the unsightly nose-blaze.
"We'll have a circus when it comes to
breakin' that critter."

Sure enough, it *was* more or less of a
circus. Perhaps the colt was at fault,
perhaps he was not. Olsen, a sullen-faced
Swede farm-hand, whose youth had been

spent in a North Sea herring-boat, and whose disposition had been matured by sundry second mates on tramp steamers, was the appropriate person selected for introducing Blue Blazes to the uses of a halter.

Judging all humans by the standard established by the mild-mannered Lafe, the colt allowed himself to be caught after small effort. But when the son of old Kate first felt a halter he threw up his head in alarm. Abruptly and violently his head was jerked down. Blue Blazes was surprised, hurt, angered. Something was bearing hard on his nose; there was something about his throat that choked.

Had he, then, been deceived? Here he was, wickedly and maliciously trapped. He jerked and slatted his head some more. This made matters worse. He was cuffed and choked. Next he tried rearing. His head was pulled savagely down, and at this point Olsen began beating him with the slack of the halter rope.

Ah, now Blue Blazes understood! They got your head and neck into that arrangement of straps and rope that they might beat you. Wild with fear he plunged desperately to right and left. Blindly he reared, pawing the air. Just as one of his hoofs struck Olsen's arm a buckle broke. The colt felt the nose-strap slide off. He was free.

A marvellous tale of fierce encounter with a devil-possessed colt did Olsen carry back to the farm-house. In proof he showed a broken halter, rope-blistered hands, and a bruised arm.

"I knew it!" said Farmer Perkins. "Knew it the minute I see them ears. He's a vicious brute, that colt, but we'll tame him."

So four of them, variously armed with whips and pitchforks, went down to the pasture and tried to drive Blue Blazes into a fence corner. But the colt was not to be cornered. From one end of the pasture to the other he raced. He had had enough of men for that day.

Next morning Farmer Perkins tried familiar strategy. Under his coat he hid a stout halter and a heavy bull whip. Then, holding a grain measure temptingly before him, he climbed the pasture fence.

In the measure were oats which he rattled seductively. Also he called mildly and persuasively. Blue Blazes was suspicious. Four times he allowed the farmer to come almost within reaching distance only to turn and bolt with a snort of alarm just at the crucial moment. At last he concluded that he must have just one taste of those oats.

"Come coltie, nice coltie," cooed the man in a strained but conciliating voice.

Blue Blazes planted himself for a sudden whirl, stretched his neck as far as possible and worked his upper lip inquiringly. The smell of the oats lured him on. Hardly had he touched his nose to the grain before the measure was dropped and he found himself roughly grabbed by the forelock. In a moment he saw the hated straps and ropes. Before he could break away the halter was around his neck and buckled firmly.

Farmer Perkins changed his tone : " Now, you damned ugly little brute, I've got you ! [Jerk] Blast your wicked hide ! [Slash] You will, will you ? [Yank] I'll larn you ! " [Slash.]

Man and colt were almost exhausted when the " lesson " was finished. It left Blue Blazes ridged with welts, trembling, fright sickened. Never again would he trust himself within reach of those men ; no, not if they offered him a whole bushel of oats.

But it was a notable victory. Vauntingly Farmer Perkins told how he had haltered the vicious colt. He was unconscious that a pair of ripe gooseberry eyes turned black with hate, that behind his broad back was shaken a futile fist.

The harness-breaking of Blue Blazes was conducted on much the same plan as his halter-taming, except that during the process he learned to use his heels. One Olsen, who has since walked with a limp, can tell you that.

Another feature of the harness-breaking came as an interruption to further bull-whip play by Farmer Perkins. It was a highly melodramatic episode in which Lafe, gripping the handle of a two-tined pitch-fork, his freckled-face greenish-white and the pupils of his eyes wide with the fear of his own daring, threatened immediate damage to the person of Farmer Perkins, unless the said Perkins dropped the whip. This Perkins did. More than that, he fled with ridiculous haste, and in craven terror; while Lafe, having given the trembling colt a parting caress, quitted the farm abruptly and for all time.

As for Blue Blazes, two days later he was sold to a travelling horse-dealer, and departed without any sorrow of farewells. In the weeks during which he trailed over the fruit district of southern Michigan in the wake of the horse-buyer, Blue Blazes learned nothing good and much that was ill. He finished the trip with raw hocks, a hoof-print on his flank, and teeth-marks on neck and withers. Horses led in a bunch do not improve in disposition.

Some of the scores the blue-roan colt paid in kind, some he did not, but he learned the game of give and take. Men and horses alike, he concluded, were against him. If he would hold his own he must be ready with teeth and hoofs. Especially he carried with him always a black, furious hatred of man in general.

So he went about with ears laid back, the whites of his eyes showing, and a bite or a kick ready in any emergency. Day by day the hate in him deepened until it became the master-passion. A quick footfall behind him was enough to send his heels flying as though they had been released by a hair-trigger. He kicked first and investigated afterward. The mere sight of a man within reaching distance roused all his ferocity.

He took a full course in vicious tricks. He learned how to crowd a man against the side of a stall, and how to reach him, when at his head, by an upward and forward stroke of the forefoot. He could kick straight behind with lightning quickness, or give the hoof a sweeping side-movement most comprehensive and unexpected. The knack of lifting the bits with the tongue and shoving them forward of the bridle-teeth came in time. It made running away a matter of choice.

When it became necessary to cause diversion he would balk. He no longer cared for whips. Physically and mentally he had become hardened to blows. Men he had ceased to fear, for most of them feared him and he knew it. He only despised and hated them. One exception Blue Blazes made. This was in favor of men and boys with red hair and freckles. Such he would not knowingly harm. A long memory had the roan.

Toward his own kind Blue Blazes bore himself defiantly. Double harness was something he loathed. One was not free to work his will on the despised driver if hampered by a pole and mate. In such cases he nipped manes and kicked under the traces until released. He had a special antipathy for gray horses and fought them on the smallest provocation, or upon none at all.

As a result Blue Blazes, while knowing no masters, had many owners, sometimes three in a single week. He began his career by filling a three months' engagement as a livery horse, but after he had run away a dozen times, wrecked several carriages, and disabled a hostler, he was sold for half his purchase price.

Then did he enter upon his wanderings in real earnest. He pulled street-cars, delivery wagons, drays and ash-carts. He was sold to unsuspecting farmers, who, when his evil traits cropped out, swapped him unceremoniously and with ingenious prevarication by the roadside. In the natural course of events he was much punished.

Up and across the southern peninsula of Michigan he drifted contentiously, growing more vicious with each encounter, more daring after each victory. In Muskegon he sent the driver of a grocery wagon to the hospital with a shoulder-bite requiring cauterization and four stitches. In Manistee he broke the small bones in the leg of a baker's large boy. In Cadillac a boarding - stable hostler struck him with an iron shovel. Blue Blazes kicked the hostler quite accurately and very suddenly through a window.

Between Cadillac and Kalaska he spent several lively weeks with farmers. Most of them tried various taming processes. Some escaped with bruises and some suffered serious injury. At Alpena he found an owner who, having read something very convincing in a horse-trainer's book, elaborately strapped the roan's legs according to diagram, and then went into the stall to wreak vengeance with a riding-whip. Blue Blazes accepted one cut, after which he crushed the avenger against the plank partition until three of the man's ribs were broken. The Alpena man was fished from under the roan's hoofs just in time to save his life.

This incident earned Blue Blazes the name of "man-killer," and it stuck. He even figured in the newspaper dispatches. "Blue Blazes, the Michigan Man-Killer," "The Ugliest Horse Alive," "Alpena's Equine Outlaw"; these were some of the head-lines. The Perkins method had borne fruit.

When purchasers for a four-legged hurricane could no longer be found, Blue Blazes was sent up the lake to an obscure little port where they have only a Tuesday and Friday steamer, and where the blue roan's record was unknown. Horses were in demand there. In fact, Blue Blazes was sold almost before he had been led down the gang-plank.

BLUE BLAZES

"Look out for him," warned the steamboat man; "he's a wicked brute."

"Oh, I've got a little job that'll soon take the cussedness out of him," said the purchaser, with a laugh.

Blue Blazes was taken down into the gloomy fore-hold of a three-masted lake schooner, harnessed securely between two long capstan bars, and set to walking in an aimless circle while a creaking cable was wound about a drum. At the other end of the cable were fastened, from time to time, squared pine-logs weighing half a ton each. It was the business of Blue Blazes to draw these timbers into the hold through a trap-door opening in the stern. There was nothing to kick save the stout bar, and there was no one to bite. Well out of reach stood a man who cracked a whip and, when not swearing forcefully, shouted "Ged-a-a-ap!"

For several uneventful days he was

forced to endure this exasperating condition of affairs with but a single break in
the monotony. This came on the first
evening, when they tried to unhook him.
The experiment ended with half a blue-
flannel shirt in the teeth of Blue Blazes
and a badly scared lumber-shover hiding
in the fore-peak. After that they put
grain and water in buckets, which they
cautiously shoved within his reach.

Of course there had to be an end to this.
In due time the Ellen B. was full of square
timbers. The Captain notified the owner
of Blue Blazes that he might take his
blankety-blanked horse out of the Ellen
B.'s fore-hold. The owner declined, and
entrenched himself behind a pure techni-
cality. The Captain had hired from him
the use of a horse; would the Captain
kindly deliver said horse to him, the owner, on the dock? It was a spirited contro-
versy, in which the horse-owner scored

several points. But the schooner captain
by no means admitted defeat.

"The Ellen B. gets under way inside
of a half hour," said he. "If you want
your blankety-blanked horse you've got
that much time to take him away."

"I stand on my rights," replied the
horse-owner. "You sail off with my property if you dare. Go ahead! Do it!
Next time the Ellen B. puts in here I'll
libel her for damages."

Yet in the face of this threat the Ellen
B. cast off her hawsers, spread her sails,
and stood up the lake bound Chicagoward
through the Straits with Blue Blazes still
on board. Not a man-jack of the crew
would venture into the fore-hold, where
Blue Blazes was still harnessed to the capstan bars.

When he had been without water or
grain for some twelve hours the wrath in
him, which had for days been growing

more intense, boiled over. Having voiced his rage in raucous squeals, he took to chewing the bridle-strap and to kicking the whiffle-tree. The deck watch gazed down at him in awe. The watch below, separated from him only by a thin partition, expressed profane disapproval of shipping such a passenger.

There was no sleep on the Ellen B. that night. About four in the morning the continued effort of Blue Blazes met with reward. The halter-strap parted, and the stout oak whiffle-tree was splintered into many pieces. For some minutes Blue Blazes explored the hold until he found the gang-plank leading upward.

His appearance on the deck of the Ellen B. caused something like a panic. The man at the wheel abandoned his post, and as he started for the cross-trees let loose a yell which brought up all hands. Blue Blazes charged them with open mouth. Not a man hesitated to jump for the rigging. The schooner's head came up into the wind, the jib-sheet blocks rattled idly and the booms swung lazily across the deck, just grazing the ears of Blue Blazes.

How long the roan might have held the deck had not his thirst been greater than his hate cannot be told. Water was what he needed most, for his throat seemed burning, and just overside was an immensity of water. So he leaped. Probably the crew of the Ellen B. believe to this day that they escaped by a miracle from a devil-possessed horse who, finding them beyond his reach, committed suicide.

But Blue Blazes had no thought of self-destruction. After swallowing as much lake water as was good for him he struck out boldly for the shore, which was not more than half a mile distant, swimming easily in the slight swell. Gaining the log-

strewn beach, he found himself at the
edge of one of those ghostly, fire-blasted
tamarack forests which cover great sec-
tions of the upper end of Michigan's
southern peninsula. At last he had escaped from the hateful bondage of man.
Contentedly he fell to cropping the coarse
beach-grass which grew at the forest's
edge.

For many long days Blue Blazes rev-
elled in his freedom, sometimes wandering for miles into the woods, sometimes
ranging the beach in search of better
pasturage. Water there was aplenty, but
food was difficult to find. He even
browsed bushes and tree-twigs. At first
he expected momentarily to see appear
one of his enemies, a man. He heard
imaginary voices in the beat of the waves,
the creaking of wind-tossed tree-tops, the
caw of crows, or in the faint whistlings of
distant steamers. He began to look sus-

piciously behind knolls and stumps. But for many miles up and down the coast was no port, and the only evidences he had of man were the sails of passing schooners, or the trailing smoke-plumes of steam-boats.

Not since he could remember had Blue Blazes been so long without feeling a whip laid over his back. Still, he was not wholly content. He felt a strange uneasiness, was conscious of a longing other than a desire for a good feed of oats. Although he knew it not, Blue Blazes, who hated men as few horses have ever hated them, was lonesome. He yearned for human society.

When at last a man did appear on the beach the horse whirled and dashed into the woods. But he ran only a short distance. Soon he picked his way back to the lake shore and gazed curiously at the intruder. The man was making a fire of

[119]

driftwood. Blue Blazes approached him cautiously. The man was bending over the fire, fanning it with his hat. In a moment he looked up.

A half minute, perhaps more, horse and man gazed at each other. Probably it was a moment of great surprise for them both. Certainly it was for the man. Suddenly Blue Blazes pricked his ears forward and whinnied. It was an unmistakable whinny of friendliness if not of glad recognition. The man on the beach had red hair—hair of the homeliest red you could imagine. Also he had eyes of the color of ripe gooseberries.

.   .   .   .

" You see," said Lafe, in explaining the matter afterward, "I was hunting for burls. I had seen 'em first when I was about sixteen. It was once when a lot of us went up on the steamer from Saginaw after black bass. We landed some-

where and went up a river into Mullet
Lake. Well, one day I got after a deer,
and he led me off so far I couldn't find
my way back to camp. I walked through
the woods for more'n a week before I
came out on the lake shore. It was
while I was tramping around that I got
into a hardwood swamp where I saw
them burls, not knowing what they were
at the time.

"When I showed up at home my step-
father was tearing mad. He licked me
good and had me sent to the reform
school. I ran away from there after a
while and struck the Perkins farm.
That's where I got to know Blue Blazes.
After my row with Perkins I drifted
about a lot until I got work in this very
furniture factory," whereupon Lafe swept
a comprehensive hand about, indicating
the sumptuously appointed office.

"Well, I worked here until I saw them

take off the cars a lot of those knots just like the ones I'd seen on the trees up in that swamp. 'What are them things?' says I to the foreman.

"'Burls,' says he.

"'Worth anything?' says I.

"'Are they?' says he. 'They're the most expensive pieces of wood you can find anywhere in this country. Them's what we saw up into veneers.'

"That was enough for me. I had a talk with the president of the company. 'If you can locate that swamp, young man,' says he, 'and it's got in it what you say it has, I'll help you to make your fortune.'

"So I started up the lake to find the swamp. That's how I come to run across Blue Blazes again. How he came to be there I couldn't guess and didn't find out for months. He was as glad to see me as I was to see him. They told me afterward that he was a man-killer. Man-killer nothing! Why, I rode that horse for over a hundred miles down the lake-shore with not a sign of a bridle on him.

"Of course, he don't seem to like other men much, and he did lay up one or two of my hostlers before I understood him. You see "—here Mr. Lafe, furniture magnate, flushed consciously—" I can't have any but red-headed men—red-headed like me, you know—about my stable, on account of Blue Blazes. Course, it's foolish, but I guess the old fellow had a tough time of it when he was young, same as I did; and now—well, he just suits me, Blue Blazes does. I'd rather ride or drive him than any thoroughbred in this country; and, by jinks, I'm bound he gets whatever he wants, even if I have to lug in a lot of red-headed men from other States."

CHIEFTAIN

A STORY OF THE HEAVY DRAUGHT SERVICE

CHIEFTAIN

A STORY OF THE HEAVY DRAUGHT SERVICE

HE was a three-quarter blood Norman, was Chieftain. You would have known that by his deep, powerful chest, his chunky neck, his substantial, shaggy-fetlocked legs. He had a family tree, registered sires, you know, and, had he wished, could have read you a pedigree reaching back to Sir Navarre (6893).

Despite all this, Chieftain was guilty of no undue pride. Eight years in the trucking business takes out of one all such nonsense. True, as a three-year-old he had given himself some airs. There was small wonder in that. He had been the boast of Keokuk County for a whole year. "We'll show 'em what we can do in Indiana," the stockmaster had said as Chieftain, his silver-white tail carefully done up in red flannel, was led aboard the cars for shipment East.

They are not unused to ton-weight horses in the neighborhood of the Bull's Head, where the great sales-stables are. Still, when Chieftain was brought out, his fine dappled coat shining like frosted steel in the sunlight, and his splendid tail, which had been done up in straw crimps over night, rippling and waving behind him, there was a great craning of necks among the buyers of heavy draughts.

"Gentlemen," the red-faced auctioneer had shouted, "here's a buster; one of the kind you read about, wide as a wagon, with a leg on each corner. There's a ton of him, a whole ton. Who'll start him at three hundred? Why, he's as good as money in the bank."

That had been Chieftain's introduction to the metropolis. But the triple-hitch is a great leveller. In single harness, even though one does pull a load, there is chance for individuality. One may toss one's head; aye, prance a bit on a nipping morning. But get between the poles of a breast-team, with a horse on either side, and a twelve-ton load at the trace-ends, and—well, one soon forgets such vanities as pride of champion sires, and one learns not to prance.

In his eight years as inside horse of breast-team No. 47, Chieftain had forgotten much about pedigree, but he had learned many other things. He had come to know the precise moment when, in easing a heavy load down an incline, it was safe to slacken away on the breeching and trot gently. He could tell, mere-

ly by glancing at a rise in the roadway,
whether a slow, steady pull was needed,
or if the time had come to stick in his
toe-calks and throw all of his two thousand
pounds on the collar. He had learned
not to fret himself into a lather about
strange noises, and not to be over-partic-
ular as to the kind of company in which
he found himself working. Even though
hitched up with a vicious Missouri Modoc
on one side and a raw, half collar-broken
Kanuck on the other, he would do his
best to steady them down to the work.
He had learned to stop at crossings when
a six-foot Broadway-squad officer held up
one finger, and to give way for no one
else. He knew by heart all the road rules
of the crowded way, and he stood for his
rights.

So, in stress of storm or quivering summer heat, did Chieftain toil between the
poles, hauling the piled-up truck, year in

[130]

He would do his best to steady them down to the work.

and year out, up and down and across the city streets. And in time he had forgotten his Norman blood, had forgotten that he was the great-grandson of Sir Navarre.

Some things there were, however, which Chieftain could not wholly forget. These memories were not exactly clear, but, vague as they were, they stuck. They had to do with fields of new grass, with the elastic feel of dew-moistened turf under one's hoofs, with the enticing smell of sweet clover in one's nostrils, the sound of gently moving leaves in one's ears, and the sense that before, as well as behind, were long hours of delicious leisure.

It was only in the afternoons that these memories troubled Chieftain. In the morning one feels fresh and strong and contented, and, when one has time for any thought at all, there are comforting reflections that in the nose-bags, swung under the truck-seat, are eight quarts of good oats, and that noon must come some time or other.

But along about three o'clock of a July day, with stabling time too far away to be thought of, when there was nothing to do but to stand patiently in the glare of the sun-baked freight-yard, while Tim and his helper loaded on case after case and barrel after barrel, then it was that Chieftain could not help thinking about the fields of new grass, and other things connected with his colt days.

Sometimes, when he was plodding doggedly over the hard pavements, with every foot-fall jarring tired muscles, he would think how nice it would be, just for a week or so, to tread again that yielding turf he had known such a long, long time ago. Then, perhaps, he would slacken just a bit on the traces, and Tim would give that queer, shrill chirrup of

his, adding, sympathetically: " Come, me
bye, come ahn!" Then Chieftain would
tighten the traces in an instant, giving his
whole attention to the business of keeping them taut and of placing each iron-
shod hoof just where was the surest footing.

In this last you may imagine there is
no knack. Perhaps you think it is done
off-hand. Well, it isn't. Ask any experienced draught-horse used to city
trucking. He will tell you that wet cob-
ble-stones, smoothed by much wear and
greased with street slime, cannot be travelled heedlessly. Either the heel or the
toe calks must find a crevice somewhere.
If they do not, you are apt to go on your
knees or slide on your haunches. Flat-
rail car-tracks give you unexpected side
slips. So do the raised rims of man-hole
covers. But when it comes to wet asphalt — your calks will not help you

there. It's just a case of nice balancing and trusting to luck.

Much, of course, depends on the man at the other end of the lines. In this particular Chieftain was fortunate, for a better driver than Tim Doyle did not handle leather for the company. Even "the old man "—the stable-boss—had been known to say as much.

Chieftain had taken a liking to Tim the first day they turned out together, when Chieftain was new to the city and to trucking. Driver Doyle's fondness for Chieftain was of slower growth. In those days there were other claimants for Tim's affections than his horses. There was a Mrs. Doyle, for instance. Sometimes Chieftain saw her when Tim drove the truck anywhere in the vicinity of the flathouse in which he lived. She would come out and look at the team, and Tim would tell what fine horses he had. There was a young Tim, too, a big, growing boy, who would now and then ride on the truck with his father.

One day—it was during Chieftain's fifth year in the service—something had happened to Mrs. Doyle. Tim had not driven for three days that time, and when he did come back he was a very sober Tim. He told Chieftain all about it, because he had no one else to tell. Soon after this young Tim, who had grown up, went away somewhere, and from that time on the friendship between old Tim and Chieftain became closer than ever. Tim spent more and more of his time at the stable, until at the end, he fixed himself a bunk in the night watchman's office and made it his home.

So, for three years or more Chieftain had always had a good-night pat on the flank from Tim, and in the morning, after the currying and rubbing, they had a lit-

tle friendly banter, in the way of love-
slaps from Tim and good-natured nosings
from Chieftain. Perhaps many of Tim's
confidences were given half in jest, and
perhaps Chieftain sometimes thought that
Tim was a bit slow in perception, but, all
in all, each understood the other, even
better than either realized.

Of course, Chieftain could not tell Tim
of all those vague longings which had to
do with new grass and springy turf, nor
could he know that Tim had similar longings. These thoughts each kept to himself. But if Chieftain was of Norman
blood, a horse whose noble sires had
ranged pasture and paddock free from
rein or trace, Tim was a Doyle whose
father and grandfather had lived close to
the good green sod, and had done their
toil in the open, with the cool and calm
of the country to soothe and revive them.

Of such delights as these both Chieftain and Tim had tasted scantily, hurriedly, in youth; and for them, in the lapses of the daily grind, both yearned, each after his own fashion.

And, each in his way, Tim and Chieftain were philosophers. As the years had come and gone, toil-filled and uneventful, the character of the man had ripened and mellowed, the disposition of the horse had settled and sweetened.

In his earlier days Tim had been ready to smash a wheel or lose one, to demand right of way with profane unction, and to back his word with whip, fist, or balehook. But he had learned to yield an inch on occasion and to use the soft word.

Chieftain, too, in his first years between the poles, had sometimes been impatient with the untrained mates who from time to time joined the team. He had taken part in mane-biting and trace-kicking, es-

pecially on days when the loads were
heavy and the flies thick, conditions which
try the best of horse tempers. But he
had steadied down into a pole-horse who
could set an example that was worth
more than all the six-foot lashes ever tied
to a whip-stock.

It was during the spring of Chieftain's
eighth year with the company that things
really began to happen. First there came
rheumatism to Tim. Trucking uses up
men as well as horses, you know. While
it is the hard work and the heavy feeding of oats which burn out the animal, it
is generally the exposure and the hard
drinking which do for the men. Tim,
however, was always moderate in his use
of liquor, so he lasted longer than most
drivers. But at one-and-forty the wearing of rain-soaked clothes called for re-
prisal. One wet May morning, after
vainly trying to hobble about the stable,

Tim, with a bottle of horse liniment under his arm, gave it up and went back to his bunk.

Team No. 47 went out that day with a new driver, a cousin of the stable-boss, who had never handled anything better than common, light-weight express horses. How Chieftain did miss Tim those next few days! The new man was slow at loading, and, to make up the time, he cut short their dinner-hour. Now it is not the wise thing to hurry horses who have just eaten eight quarts of oats. The team finished the day well blown, and in a condition generally bad. Next day the new man let the off horse stumble, and there was a pair of barked knees to be doctored.

Matters went from bad to worse, until on the fourth day came the climax. Sludge acid is an innocent-appearing liquid which sometimes stands in pools

near gas-works. Good drivers know
enough to avoid it. It is bad for the
hoofs. The new man still had many
things to learn, and this happened to be
one of them. In the morning Team 47
was disabled. The company's veterinary
looked at the spongy hoofs and remarked
to the stable-boss: "About three weeks
on the farm will fix 'em all right, I guess;
but I should advise you to chuck that
new driver out of the window; he's too
expensive for us."

That was how Chieftain's yearnings
happened to be gratified at last. The
company, it seems, has a big farm, somewhere "up State," to which disabled
horses are sent for rest and recuperation.
Invalided drivers must look out for themselves. You can get a hundred truck
drivers by hanging out a sign: good
draught horses are to be had only for a
price.

CHIEFTAIN

Chieftain and Tim parted with mutual misgivings. To a younger horse the long ride in the partly open stock-car might have been a novelty, but to Chieftain, accustomed to ferries and the sight of all manner of wheeled things, it was without new sensations.

At the end of the ride—ah, that was different. There were the sweet, fresh fields, the springy green turf, the trees—all just as he had dreamed a hundred times. Halterless and shoe-freed, Chieftain pranced about the pasture for all the world like a two-year-old. With head and tail up he ranged the field. He even tried a roll on the grass. Then, when he was tired, he wandered about, nibbling now and then at a tempting bunch of grass, but mainly exulting in his freedom. There were other company horses in the field, but most of them were busy grazing. Each was disabled in some way.

One was half foundered, one had a leg-sprain, another swollen joints ; but hoof complaints, such as toe-cracks, quarter-cracks, brittle feet, and the like, were the most frequent ills. They were not a cheerful lot, and they were unsociable.

Chieftain went ambling off by himself, and in due time made acquaintance with a rather gaunt, weather-beaten sorrel who hung his head lonesomely over the fence from an adjoining pasture. He seemed grateful for the notice taken of him by the big Norman, and soon they were the best of friends. For hours they stood with their muzzles close together or their necks crossed in fraternal fashion, swapping horse gossip after the manner of their kind.

The sorrel, it appeared, was farm-bred and farm-reared. He knew little or nothing of pavements and city hauling. All his years had been spent in the country. In spite of his bulging ribs and unkempt coat Chieftain almost envied him. What a fine thing it must be to live as the sorrel lived, to crop the new grass, to feel the turf under your feet, and to drink, instead of the hard stuff one gets from the hydrant, the soft sweet brook water, to drink it standing fetlock deep in the hoof-soothing mud! But the sorrel was lacking in enthusiasm for country life.

About the fifth day of his rustication the sharp edge of Chieftain's appreciation became dulled. He discovered that pasture life was wanting in variety. Also he missed his oats. When one has been accustomed to twenty-four quarts a day, and hay besides, grass seems a mild substitute. Graze industriously as he would, it was hard to get enough. The sorrel, however, was sure Chieftain would get used to all that.

In time, of course, the talk turned to
the pulling of heavy loads. The sorrel
mentioned the yanking of a hay-rick,
laden with two tons of clover, from the
far meadow lot to the barn. Two tons!
Chieftain snorted in mild disdain. Had
not his team often swung down Broadway with sixteen tons on the truck? To
be sure, narrow tires and soft-going made
a difference.

The country horse suggested that dragging a breaking plough through old sod
was strenuous employment. Yes, it
might be, but had the sorrel ever tightened the traces for a dash up a ferry
bridgeway when the tide was out? No,
the sorrel had done his hauling on land.
He had never ridden on boats. He had
heard them, though. They were noisy
things, almost as noisy as an old Buckeye
mower going over a stony field.

Noise! Would the sorrel like to know

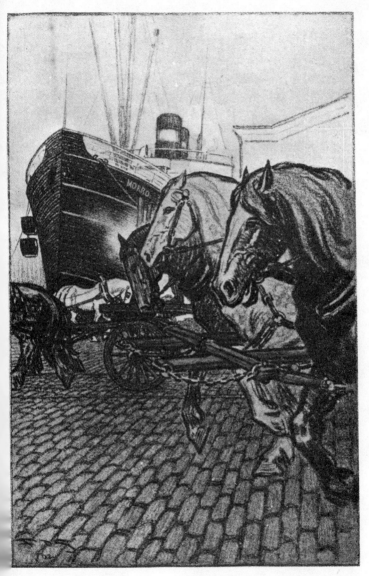

Then let him snake a truck down West Street.

what noise really was? Then let him be hooked into a triple Boston backing hitch and snake a truck down West Street, with the whiffle-trees slatting in front of him, the spreader-bar rapping jig time on the poles, and the gongs of street-cars and automobiles and fire-engines and ambulances all going at once. Noise? Let him mix in a Canal Street jam or back up for a load on a North River pier!

And as Chieftain recalled these things the contrast of the pasture's oppressive stillness to the lively roar of the familiar streets came home to him. Who was taking his place between the poles of Team 47? Had they put one of those cheeky Clydes in his old stall? He would not care to lose that stall. It was the best on the second floor. It had a window in it, and Sundays he could see everything that went on in the street below. He could even look into the front rooms of the tenements across the way. There was a little girl over there who interested Chieftain greatly. She was trying to raise some sort of a flower in a tin can which she kept on the window-ledge. She often waved her hand at Chieftain.

Then there was poor Tim Doyle. Good old Tim! Where was another driver like him? He made you work, Tim did, but he looked out for you all the time. Always on the watch, was Tim, for galled spots, chafing sores, hoof-pricks, and things like that. If he could get them he would put on fresh collar-pads every week. And how carefully he would cover you up when you were on the forward end of a ferryboat in stormy weather. No tossing the blanket over your back from Tim. No, sir! It was always doubled about your neck and chest, just where you most need protection when you're steaming hot and the wind is raw. How many drivers warmed the bits on a cold morning or rinsed out your mouth in hot weather? Who, but Tim could drive a breast team through a——

But just here Chieftain heard a shrill, familiar whistle, and in a moment, with as much speed as his heavy build allowed, he was making his way across the field to where a short, stocky man with a broad grin cleaving his face, was climbing the pasture-fence. It was Tim Doyle himself.

Tim, it seems, had so bothered the stable-boss with questions about the farm, its location, distance from the city, and general management, that at last that autocrat had said: "See here, Doyle, if you want to go up there just say so and I'll send you as car hostler with the next batch. I'll give you a note to the farm superintendent. Guess he'll let you hang around for a week or so."

" I'll go up as hostler," said Tim, " but you just say in that there note that Tim Doyle pays his own way after he gets there."

In that way it was settled. For some four days Tim appeared to enjoy it greatly. Most of his time he spent sitting on the pasture-fence, smoking his pipe and watching the grazing horses. To Chieftain alone he brought great bunches of clover.

About the fifth day Tim grew restive. He had examined Chieftain's hoofs and pronounced them well healed, but the superintendent said that it would be a week before he should be ready to send another lot of horses back to the city.

" How far is it by road? " asked Tim.

" Oh, two hundred miles or so," said the superintendent.

CHIEFTAIN

" Why not let me take Chieftain down
that way? It'd be cheaper'n shippin'
him, an' do him good."

The superintendent only laughed and
said he would ship Chieftain with the
others, when he was ready.

That evening Tim sat on the bench before the farmhouse and smoked his pipe
until everyone else had gone to bed. The
moon had risen, big and yellow. In a
pond behind the stables it seemed as if ten
thousand frogs had joined in one grand
chorus. They were singing their mating
song, if you know what that is. It is not
altogether a cheerful or harmonious effort. Next to the soughing of a November wind it is, perhaps, the most dismally
lonesome sound in nature.

For two hours Tim Doyle smoked and
thought and listened. Then he knocked
the ashes out of his pipe and decided that
he had been long enough in the country.

He would walk to the station, two miles away, and take the midnight train to the city. As he went down the farm road skirting the pasture he saw in the moonlight the sheds where the horses went at night for shelter. Moved by some sudden whim, he stopped and whistled. A moment later a big horse appeared from under the shed and came toward him, neighing gratefully. It was Chieftain.

"Well, Chieftain, me bye, I'll be lavin' ye for a spell. But I'll have yer old stall ready against yer comin' back. Good-by, laddie," and with this Tim patted Chieftain on the nose and started down the road. He had gone but a few steps when he heard Chieftain whinny. Tim stopped irresolutely, and then went on. Again came the call of the horse. There was no misunderstanding its meaning. Tim walked back to the fence.

In the morning the farm superintend-

ent found on the door-sill a roughly pen-
cilled note which read :

" Hav goan bak to the sitty P S chefe-
tun warnted to goe so I tuk him. Tim
Doyle."

They were ten days on the road, ten
delightful days of irresponsible vagabond-
ism. Sometimes Tim rode on Chieftain's
back and sometimes he walked beside
him. At night they took shelter in any
stable that was handy. Tim invested in
a bridle and saddle blanket. Also he
bought oats and hay for Chieftain. The
big Norman followed his own will, stopping to graze by the roadside whenever
he wished. Together they drank from
brooks and springs. Between them was
perfect comradeship. Each was in holi-
day mood and each enjoyed the outing
to the fullest. As they passed through
towns they attracted no little attention,
for outside of the city 2,000-pound horses

are seldom seen, and there were many ad-
mirers of Chieftain's splendid proportions.
Tim had many offers from shrewd horse-
dealers.

"Ye would, eh? A whole hundred
dollars!" Tim would answer with fine
sarcasm. "Now, wouldn't that be too
much, don't ye think? My, my, what a
generous mon it is! G'wan, Chieftain, er
Mister Car-na-gy here'll be after givin' us
a lib'ry."

Chieftain, and Tim, too, for that matter, were nearer actual freedom than ever
before. For years the big Norman had
used his magnificent muscles only for
straining at the traces. He had trod only
the hard pavements. Now, he put forth
his glorious strength at leisure, moving
along the pleasant country roads at his
own gait, and being guided only when a
turning was to be made.

Fine as it all was, however, as they

drew near to the city both horse and driver became eager to reach their old quarters. Tim was, for he has said so. As for Chieftain—let the stable-boss, who knows horse-nature better than most men know themselves, tell that part of the story.

" Bigger lunatics than them two, Tim Doyle and old Chieftain, I never set eyes on," he says. "I was standin' down here by the double doors watchin' some of the day-teams unhook when I looks up the street on a sudden. An' there, tail an' head up like he was a 'leven-hundred-pound Kentucky hunter 'stead of heavy-weight draught, comes that old Chieftain, a whinnyin' like a three-year-old. An' on his back, mind you, old Tim Doyle, grinnin' away 'sif he was Tod Sloan fin-ishin' first at the Brooklyn Handicap. Tickled? I never see a horse show anything so plain in all my life. He just

[153]

streaked it up that runway and into his old stall like he was a prodigal son come back from furren parts.

"Yes, Tim he's out on the truck with his old team. Tim don't have to drive nowadays, you know. Brother of his that was in the contractin' business died about three months ago an' left Tim quite a pile. Tim, he says he guesses the money won't take no hurt in the bank and that some day, when he an' Chieftain git ready to retire, maybe it'll come in handy."

BARNACLES

WHO MUTINIED FOR GOOD CAUSE

BARNACLES

WHO MUTINIED FOR GOOD CAUSE

WITH his coming to Sculpin Point there was begun for Barnacles the most surprising period of a more or less useful career which had been filled with unusual equine activities. For Barnacles was a horse, a white horse of unguessed breed and uncertain age.

Most likely it was not, but it may have been, Barnacles's first intimate connection with an affair of the heart. Said affair was between Captain Bastabol Bean, owner and occupant of Sculpin Point, and Mrs. Stashia Buckett, the unlamenting relict of the late Hosea Buckett.

Mrs. Buckett it was who induced Captain Bastabol Bean to purchase a horse. Captain Bean, you will understand, had just won the affections of the plump Mrs. Buckett. Also he had, with a sailor's ignorance of feminine ways, presumed to settle offhand the details of the coming nuptials.

"I'll sail over in the dory Monday afternoon," said he, "and take you back with me to Sculpin Point. You can have your dunnage sent over later by team. In the evenin' we'll have a shore chaplain come 'round an' make the splice."

"Cap'n Bean," replied the rotund Stashia, "we won't do any of them things, not one."

"Wha-a-at!" gasped the Captain.

"Have you ever been married, Cap'n Bean?"

"N-n-no, my dear."

" Well, I have, and I guess I know how it ought to be done. You'll have the minister come here, and here *you'll* come to marry me. You won't come in no dory, either. Catch me puttin' my two hundred an' thirty pounds into a little boat like that. You'll drive over here with a horse, like a respectable person, and you'll drive back with me, by land and past Sarepta Tucker's house so's she can see."

Now for more than thirty years Bastabol Bean, as master of coasting schooners up and down the Atlantic seaboard, had given orders. He had taken none, except the formal directions of owners. He did not propose to begin taking them now, not even from such an altogether charming person as Stashia Buckett. This much he said. Then he added :

" Stashia, I give in about coming here to marry you ; that seems no more than fair. But I'll come in a dory and you'll go back in a dory."

"Then you needn't come at all, Cap'n Bastabol Bean."

Argue and plead as he might, this was her ultimatum.

"But, Stashia, I 'ain't got a horse, never owned one an' never handled one, and you know it," urged the Captain.

"Then it's high time you had a horse and knew how to drive him. Besides, if I go to Sculpin Point I shall want to come to the village once in a while. I sha'n't sail and I sha'n't walk. If I can't ride like a lady I don't go to the Point."

The inevitable happened. Captain Bean promised to buy a horse next day. Hence his visit to Jed Holden and his introduction to Barnacles, as the Captain immediately named him.

As one who inspects an unfamiliar object, Captain Bean looked dazedly at Bar-

nacles. At the same time Barnacles inspected the Captain. With head lowered to knee level, with ears cocked
forward, nostrils sniffing and under-lip
twitching almost as if he meant to laugh,
Barnacles eyed his prospective owner.
In common with most intelligent horses,
he had an almost human way of expressing curiosity.

Captain Bean squirmed under the gaze
of Barnacles's big, calm eyes for a moment, and then shifted his position.

"What in time does he want anyway,
Jed?" demanded the Captain.

"Wants to git acquainted, that's all,
Cap'n. Mighty knowin' hoss, he is.
Now some hosses don't take notice of
anything. They're jest naturally dumb.
Then agin you'll find hosses that seem
to know every blamed word you say.
Them's the kind of hosses that's wuth
havin."

" S'pose he knows all the ropes, Jed? "

" I should say he did, Cap'n.   If there's anything that hoss ain't done in his day I don't know what 'tis.   Near's I can find out he's tried every kind of work, in or out of traces, that you could think of."

"Sho!"   The Captain was now looking at the old white horse in an interested manner.

" Yes, sir, that's a remarkable hoss," continued the now enthusiastic Mr. Holden.   "He's been in the cavalry service, for he knows the bugle calls like a book.   He's travelled with a circus— ain't no more afraid of elephants than I be.   He's run on a fire engine—know that 'cause he wants to chase old Reliance every time she turns out.   He's been a street-car hoss, too.   You jest ring a door gong behind him twice an' see how quick he'll dig in his toes.   The feller I got him off'n said he knew of his havin' been used on a milk wagon, a pedler's cart and a hack. Fact is, he's an all round worker."

" Must be some old by your tell," suggested the Captain. " Sure his timbers are all sound? "

" Dun'no' 'bout his timbers, Cap'n, but as fer wind an' limb you won't find a sounder hoss, of his age, in this county. Course, I'm not sellin' him fer a four-year-old. But for your work, joggin' from the P'int into the village an' back once or twice a week, I sh'd say he was jest the ticket; an' forty-five, harness an' all as he stands, is dirt cheap."

Again Captain Bean tried to look critically at the white horse, but once more he met that calm, curious gaze and the attempt was hardly a success. However, the Captain squinted solemnly over Barnacles's withers and remarked:

" Yes, he has got some good lines, as

you say, though you wouldn't hardly call him clipper built. Not much sheer for-'ard an' a leetle too much aft, eh?"

At this criticism Jed snorted mirth-fully.

"Oh, I s'pose he's all right," quickly added the Captain. "Fact is, I ain't never paid much attention to horses, bein' on the water so much. You're sure he'll mind his helm, Jed?"

"Oh, he'll go where you p'int him."

"Won't drag anchor, will he?"

"Stand all day if you'll let him."

"Well, Jed, I'm ready to sign articles, I guess."

It was about noon that a stable-boy de-livered Barnacles at Sculpin Point. His arrival caused Lank Peters to suspend peeling the potatoes for dinner and de-mand explanation.

"Who's the hoss for, Cap'n?" asked Lank.

BARNACLES

It was a question that Captain Bean had been dreading for two hours. When he had given up coasting, bought the strip of Massachusetts seashore known as Sculpin Point, built a comfortable cottage on it and settled down within sight and sound of the salt water, he had brought with him Lank Peters, who for a dozen years had presided over the galley in the Captain's ship.

More than a mere sea-cook was Lank Peters to Captain Bean. He was confidential friend, advising philosopher, and mate of Sculpin Point. Yet from Lank had the Captain carefully concealed all knowledge of his affair with the Widow Buckett. The time of confession was at hand.

In his own way and with a directness peculiar to all his acts, did Captain Bean admit the full sum of his rashness, adding, thoughtfully: " I s'pose you won't have to do much cookin' after Stashia comes; but you'll still be mate, Lank, and there'll be plenty to keep you busy on the P'int."

Quietly and with no show of emotion, as befitted a sea-cook and a philosopher, Melankthon Peters heard these revelations. If he had his prejudices as to the wisdom or folly of marrying widows, he said no word. But in the matter of Barnacles he felt more free to express something of his uneasiness.

"I didn't ship for no hostler, Cap'n, an' I guess I'll make a poor fist at it, but I'll do my best," he said.

"Guess we'll manage him between us, Lank," cheerfully responded the Captain. "I ain't got much use for horses myself; but as I said, Stashia, she's down on boats."

"Kinder sot in her idees, ain't she, Cap'n?" insinuated Lank.

"Well, kinder," the Captain admitted.

Lank permitted himself to chuckle guardedly. Captain Bastabol Bean, as an innumerable number of sailor-men had learned, was a person who generally had his own way. Intuitively the Captain understood that Lank had guessed of his surrender. A grim smile was barely suggested by the wrinkles about his mouth and eyes.

"Lank," he said, "the Widow Buckett an' me had some little argument over this horse business an'—an'—I give in. She told me flat she wouldn't come to the P'int if I tried to fetch her by water in the dory. Well, I want Stashia mighty bad; for she's a fine woman, Lank, a mighty fine woman, as you'll say when you know her. So I promised to bring her home by land and with a horse. I'm bound to do it, too. But by time!" Here the Captain suddenly slapped his

knee. "I've just been struck with a no-
tion. Lank, I'm going to see what you
think of it."

For an hour Captain and mate sat in
the sun, smoked their pipes and talked
earnestly. Then they separated. Lank
began a close study of Barnacles's complicated rigging. The Captain tramped off
toward the village.

Late in the afternoon the Captain returned riding in a sidebar buggy with a
man. Behind the buggy they towed a
skeleton lumber wagon—four wheels connected by an extension pole. The man
drove away in the sidebar leaving the
Captain and the lumber wagon.

Barnacles, who had been moored to a
kedge-anchor, watched the next day's
proceedings with interest. He saw the
Captain and Lank drag up from the
beach the twenty-foot dory and hoist it
up between the wheels. Through the

forward part of the keelson they bored a
hole for the king-bolt. With nut-bolts
they fastened the stern to the rear axle,
adding some very seamanlike lashings to
stay the boat in place. As finishing
touches they painted the upper strakes of
the dory white, giving to the lower part
and to the running-gear of the cart a coat
of sea-green.

Barnacles was experienced, but a vehicle such as this amphibious product of
Sculpin Point he had never before seen.
With ears pointed and nostrils palpitating
from curiosity, he was led up to the boat-
bodied wagon. Reluctantly he backed under the raised shafts. The practice-hitch
was enlivened by a monologue, on the
part of Captain Bean, which ran something like this :

" Now, Lank, pass aft that backstay
[the trace] and belay ; no, not there !
Belay to that little yard-arm [whiffle-

tree]. Got it through the lazy-jack
[trace-bearer]? Now reeve your jib-
sheets [lines] through them dead-eyes
[hame rings] and pass 'em aft. Now
where in Tophet does this thingumbob
[holdback] go? Give it a turn around
the port bowsprit [shaft]. There, guess
everything's taut."

The Captain stood off to take an ad-
miring glance at the turnout.

"She's down by the bow some, Lank,
but I guess she'll lighten when we get
aboard. See what you think."

Lank's inspection caused him to medi-
tate and scratch his head. Finally he
gave his verdict: "From midships aft she
looks as trim as a liner, but from midships
for'ard she looks scousy, like a Norwegian
tramp after a v'yage round The Horn."

"Color of old Barnacles don't suit, eh?
No, it don't, that's so. But I couldn't
find no green an' white horse, Lank."

BARNACLES

"Couldn't we paint him up a leetle, Cap'n?"

"By Sancho, I never thought of that!" exclaimed Captain Bean. "Course we can; git a string an' we'll strike a water-line on him."

With no more ado than as if the thing was quite usual, the preparations for carrying out this indignity were begun. Perhaps the victim thought it a new kind of grooming, for he made no protest. Half an hour later old Barnacles, from about the middle of his barrel down to his shoes, was painted a beautiful sea-green. Like some resplendent marine monster shone the lower half of him. It may have been a trifle bizarre, but, with the sun on the fresh paint, the effect was unmistakably striking. Besides, his color now matched that of the dory's with startling exactness.

"That's what I call real ship-shape,"

declared Captain Bean, viewing the result. "Got any more notions, Lank?"

"Strikes me we ought to ship a mast so's we could rig a sprit-sail in case the old horse should give out, Cap'n."

"We'll do it, Lank; fust rate idee!"

So a mast and sprit-sail were rigged in the dory. Also the lines were length-ened with rope, that the Captain might steer from the stern sheets.

"She's as fine a land-goin' craft as ever I see anywhere," said the Captain, which was certainly no extravagant statement.

How Captain Bean and his mate steered the equipage from Sculpin Point to the village, how they were cheered and hooted along the route, how they ran into the yard of the Metropolitan Livery Stable as a port of refuge, how the Captain escaped to the home of Widow Buckett, how the "splicin'" was accomplished—these are details which must be slighted.

BARNACLES

The climax came when the newly made Mrs. Bastabol Buckett Bean, her plump hand resting affectionately on the sleeve of the Captain's best blue broad-cloth coat, said, cooingly : " Now, Cap'n, I'm ready to drive to Sculpin Point."

" All right, Stashia, Lank's waitin' for us at the front door with the craft."

At first sight of the boat on wheels Mrs. Bean could do no more than attempt, by means of indistinct ejacula-tion, to express her obvious emotion. She noted the grinning crowd of villagers, Sarepta Tucker among them. She saw the white and green dory with its mast, and with Lank, villainously smiling, at the top of a step-ladder which had been leaned against the boat; she saw the green wheels, and the verdant gorgeous-ness of Barnacles's lower half. For a moment she gazed at the fantastic equi-page and spoke not. Then she slammed

the front door with an indignant bang,
marched back into the sitting-room and
threw herself on the haircloth sofa with
an abandon that carried away half a
dozen springs.

For the first hour she reiterated, between vast sobs, that Captain Bean was a
soulless wretch, that she would never set
foot on Sculpin Point, and that she
would die there on the sofa rather than
ride in such an outlandish rig.

Many a time had Captain Bean weath-
ered Hatteras in a southeaster, but never
had he met such a storm of feminine fury
as this. However, he stood by like a
man, putting in soothing words of explanation and endearment whenever a lull
gave opportunity.

Toward evening the storm spent itself.
The disturbed Stashia became somewhat
calm. Eventually she laughed hysteri-
cally at the Captain's arguments, and in

the end she compromised. Not by day would she enter the dory wagon, but late in the evening she would swallow her pride and go, just to please the Captain.

Thus it was that soon after ten o'clock, when the village folks had laughed their fill and gone away, the new Mrs. Bean climbed the step-ladder, bestowed herself unhandily on the midship thwart and, with Lank on lookout in the bow, and Captain Bean handling the reins from the stern sheets, the honeymoon chariot got under way.

By the time they reached the Shell Road the gait of the dejected Barnacles had dwindled to a deliberate walk which all of Lank's urgings could not hasten. It was a soft July night with a brisk off-shore breeze and the moon had come up out of the sea to silver the highway and lay a strip of milk-white carpet over the waves.

"Ahoy there, Lank!" shouted the bridegroom. "Can't we do better'n this? Ain't hardly got steerage-way on her."

"Can't budge him, Cap'n. Hadn't we better shake out the sprit-sail; wind's fair abeam."

"Yes, shake it out, Lank."

Mrs. Bean's feeble protest was unheeded. As the night wind caught the sail and rounded it out the flapping caused old Barnacles to cast an investigating glance behind him. One look at the terrible white thing which loomed menacingly above him was enough. He decided to bolt. Bolt he did to the best of his ability, all obstacles being considered. A down grade in the Shell Road, where it dipped toward the shore, helped things along. Barnacles tightened the traces, the sprit-sail did its share, and in an amazingly short time the odd vehicle was spinning toward Sculpin Point at a ten-knot

gait. Desperately Mrs. Bean gripped the
gunwale and lustily she screamed:

"Whoa, whoa! Stop him, Captain,
stop him! He'll smash us all to
pieces!"

"Set right still, Stashia, an' trim ship.
I've got the helm," responded the Captain, who had set his jaws and was tugging at the rope lines.

"Breakers ahead, sir!" shouted Lank
at this juncture.

Sure enough, not fifty yards ahead, the
Shell Road turned sharply away from the
edge of the beach to make a detour by
which Sculpin Point was cut off.

"I see 'em, Lank."

"Think we can come about, Cap'n?"
asked Lank, anxiously.

"Ain't goin to try, Lank. I'm layin' a
straight course for home. Stand by to
bail."

How they could possibly escape capsiz-

ing Lank could not understand until, just
as Barnacles was about to make the turn,
he saw the Captain tighten the right-
hand rein until it was as taut as a weather-
stay. Of necessity Barnacles made no
turn, and there was no upset. Something equally exciting happened, though.

Leaving the road with a speed which
he had not equalled since the days when
he had figured in the " The Grand Hippodrome Races," his sea-green legs quick-
ened by the impetus of the affair behind
him, Barnacles cleared the narrow strip of
beach-grass at a jump. Another leap and
he was hock deep in the surf. Still another, and he split a roller with his white
nose.

With a dull chug, a resonant thump,
and an impetuous splash the dory entered
its accustomed element, lifting some three
gallons of salt water neatly over the bows.
Lank ducked. The unsuspecting Stashia

did not, and the flying brine struck fairly under her ample chin.

"Ug-g-g-gh! Oh! Oh! H-h-h-elp!" spluttered the startled bride, and tried to get on her feet.

"Sit down!" roared Captain Bean. Vehemently Stashia sat.

"W-w-w-we'll all b-b-be d-d-drowned, drowned!" she wailed.

"Not much we won't, Stashia. We're all right now, and we ain't goin' to have our necks broke by no fool horse, either. Trim in the sheet, Lank, an' then take that bailin' scoop." The Captain was now calmly confident and thoroughly at home.

Drenched, cowed and trembling, the newly made Mrs. Bean clung despairingly to the thwart, fully as terrified as the plunging Barnacles, who struck out wildly with his green legs, and snorted every time a wave hit him. But the lines

held up his head and kept his nose pointing straight for the little beach on Sculpin
Point, perhaps a quarter of a mile distant.

Somewhat heavy weather the deep-
laden dory made of it, and in spite of
Lank's vigorous bailing the water sloshed
around Mrs. Bean's boot-tops, yet in time
the sail and Barnacles brought them
safely home.

" 'Twa'n't exactly the kind of honeymoon trip I'd planned, Stashia," commented the Captain, as he and Lank
steadied the bride's dripping bulk down
the step-ladder, "and we did do some
sailin', spite of ourselves; but we had a
horse in front an' wheels under us all the
way, just as I promised."

BLACK EAGLE

WHO ONCE RULED THE RANGES

BLACK EAGLE

WHO ONCE RULED THE RANGES

OF his sire and dam there is no record. All that is known is that he was raised on a Kentucky stock farm. Perhaps he was a son of Hanover, but Hanoverian or no, he was a thoroughbred. In the ordinary course of events he would have been tried out with the other three-year olds for the big meet on Churchill Downs. In the hands of a good trainer he might have carried to victory the silk of some great stable and had his name printed in the sporting almanacs to this day.

But there was about Black Eagle nothing ordinary, either in his blood or in his career. He was born for the part he played. So at three, instead of being entered in his class at Louisville, it happened that he was shipped West, where his fate waited.

No more comely three year old ever took the Santa Fé trail. Although he stood but thirteen hands and tipped the beam at scarcely twelve hundred weight, you might have guessed him to be taller by two hands. The deception lay in the way he carried his shapely head and in the manner in which his arched neck tapered from the well-placed shoulders.

A horseman would have said that he had a " perfect barrel," meaning that his ribs were well rounded. His very gait was an embodied essay on graceful pride. As for his coat, save for a white star just in the middle of his forehead, it was as black and sleek as the nap on a new silk

[184]

hat. After a good rubbing he was so shiny that at a distance you might have thought him starched and ironed and newly come from the laundry.

His arrival at Bar L Ranch made no great stir, however. They were not connoisseurs of good blood and sleek coats at the Bar L outfit. They were busy folks who most needed tough animals that could lope off fifty miles at a stretch. They wanted horses whose education included the fine art of knowing when to settle back on the rope and dig in toes. It was not a question as to how fast you could do your seven furlongs. It was more important to know if you could make yourself useful at a round-up.

"'Nother bunch o' them green Eastern horses," grumbled the ranch boss as the lot was turned into a corral. "But that black fellow'd make a rustler's mouth water, eh, Lefty?" In answer to which

the said Lefty, being a man little given
to speech, grunted.

"We'll brand 'em in the mornin',"
added the ranch boss.

Now most steers and all horses object
to the branding process. Even the
spiritless little Indian ponies, accustomed
to many ingenious kinds of abuse, rebel
at this. A meek-eyed mule, on whom
humility rests as an all-covering robe,
must be properly roped before submitting.

In branding they first get a rope over
your neck and shut off your wind. Then
they trip your feet by roping your forelegs while you are on the jump. This
brings you down hard and with much
abruptness. A cowboy sits on your head
while others pin you to the ground from
various vantage-points. Next someone
holds a red-hot iron on your rump until it
has sunk deep into your skin. That is
branding.

BLACK EAGLE

Well, this thing they did to the black thoroughbred, who had up to that time felt not so much as the touch of a whip. They did it, but not before a full dozen cow-punchers had worked themselves into such a fury of exasperation that no shred of picturesque profanity was left unused among them.

Quivering with fear and anger, the black, as soon as the ropes were taken off, dashed madly about the corral looking in vain for a way of escape from his torturers. Corrals, however, are built to resist just such dashes. The burn of a branding iron is supposed to heal almost immediately. Cowboys will tell you that a horse is always more frightened than hurt during the operation, and that the day after he feels none the worse.

All this you need not credit. A burn is a burn, whether made purposely with a branding iron or by accident in any other way. The scorched flesh puckers and smarts. It hurts every time a leg is moved. It seems as if a thousand needles were playing a tattoo on the exposed surface. Neither is this the worst of the business. To a high-strung animal the roping, throwing, and burning is a tremendous nervous shock. For days after branding a horse will jump and start, quivering with expectant agony, at the slightest cause.

It was fully a week before the black thoroughbred was himself again. In that time he had conceived such a deep and lasting hatred for all men, cowboys in particular, as only a high-spirited, blue-blooded horse can acquire. With deep contempt he watched the scrubby little cow ponies as they doggedly carried about those wild, fierce men who threw their circling, whistling, hateful ropes, who wore such big, sharp spurs and who were viciously handy in using their raw-hide quirts.

So when a cowboy put a breaking-bit into the black's mouth there was another lively scene. It was somewhat confused, this scene, but at intervals one could make out that the man, holding stubbornly to mane and forelock, was being slatted and slammed and jerked, now with his feet on the ground, now thrown high in the air and now dangling perilously and at various angles as the stallion raced away.

In the end, of course, came the whistle of the choking, foot-tangling ropes, and the black was saddled. For a fierce half hour he took punishment from bit and spur and quirt. Then, although he gave it up, it was not that his spirit was broken, but because his wind was gone. Quite passively he allowed himself to be ridden out on the prairie to where the herds were grazing.

Undeceived by this apparent docility, the cowboy, when the time came for him to bunk down under the chuck wagon for a few hours of sleep, tethered his mount quite securely to a deep-driven stake. Before the cattleman had taken more than a round dozen of winks the black had tested his tether to the limit of his strength. The tether stood the test. A cow pony might have done this much. There he would have stopped. But the black was a Kentucky thoroughbred, blessed with the inherited intelligence of noble sires, some of whom had been household pets. So he investigated the tether at close range.

Feeling the stake with his sensitive upper lip he discovered it to be firm as a rock. Next he backed away and wrenched tentatively at the halter until convinced that the throat strap was thoroughly sound. His last effort must have been an inspiration. Attacking the taut buckskin rope with his teeth he worked diligently until he had severed three of the four strands. Then he gathered himself for another lunge. With a snap the rope parted and the black dashed away into the night, leaving the cowboy snoring confidently by the camp-fire.

All night he ran, on and on in the darkness, stopping only to listen tremblingly to the echo of his own hoofs and to sniff suspiciously at the crouching shadows of innocent bushes. By morning he had left the Bar L outfit many miles behind, and when the red sun rolled up over the edge of the prairie he saw that he was alone in a field that stretched unbroken to the circling sky-line.

Not until noon did the runaway black scent water. Half mad with thirst he dashed to the edge of a muddy little stream and sucked down a great draught.

As he raised his head he saw standing poised above him on the opposite bank, with ears laid menacingly flat and nostrils aquiver in nervous palpitation, a buckskin-colored stallion.

Snorting from fright the black wheeled and ran. He heard behind him a shrill neigh of challenge and in a moment the thunder of many hoofs. Looking back he saw fully a score of horses, the buckskin stallion in the van, charging after him. That was enough. Filling his great lungs with air he leaped into such a burst of speed that his pursuers soon tired of the hopeless chase. Finding that he was no longer followed the black grew curious. Galloping in a circle he gradually approached the band. The horses had settled down to the cropping of buffalo grass, only the buckskin stallion, who had taken a position on a little knoll, remaining on guard.

The surprising thing about this band was that each and every member seemed riderless. Not until he had taken long up-wind sniffs was the thoroughbred convinced of this fact. When certain on this point he cantered toward the band, sniffing inquiringly. Again the buckskin stallion charged, ears back, eyes gleaming wickedly and snorting defiantly. This time the black stood his ground until the buckskin's teeth snapped savagely within a few inches of his throat. Just in time did he rear and swerve. Twice more— for the paddock-raised black was slow to understand such behavior—the buckskin charged. Then the black was roused into aggressiveness.

There ensued such a battle as would have brought delight to the brute soul of a Nero. With fore-feet and teeth the two stallions engaged, circling madly about on their hind legs, tearing up great clods

of turf, biting and striking as opportunity
offered. At last, by a quick, desperate
rush, the buckskin caught the thoroughbred fairly by the throat. Here the affair
would have ended had not the black stallion, rearing suddenly on his muscle-ridged
haunches and lifting his opponent's fore-
quarters clear of the ground, showered on
his enemy such a rain of blows from his
iron-shod feet that the wild buckskin
dropped to the ground, dazed and van-
quished.

Standing over him, with all the fierce
pride of a victorious gladiator showing in
every curve of his glistening body, the
black thoroughbred trumpeted out a sten-
torian call of defiance and command. The
band, that had watched the struggle from
a discreet distance, now came galloping
in, whinnying in friendly fashion.

Black Eagle had won his first fight.
He had won the leadership. By right of

might he was now chief of this free company of plains rangers. It was for him to lead whither he chose, to pick the place and hour of grazing, the time for watering, and his to guard his companions from all dangers.

As for the buckskin stallion, there remained for him the choice of humbly following the new leader or of limping off alone to try to raise a new band. Being a worthy descendant of the chargers which the men of Cortez rode so fearlessly into the wilds of the New World he chose the latter course, and, having regained his senses, galloped stiffly toward the north, his bruised head lowered in defeat.

Some months later Arizona stockmen began to hear tales of a great band of wild horses, led by a magnificent black stallion which was fleeter than a scared coyote. There came reports of much mischief. Cattle were stampeded by day, calves trampled to death, and steers scattered far and wide over the prairie. By night bunches of tethered cow ponies disappeared. The exasperated cowboys could only tell that suddenly out of the darkness had swept down on their quiet camps an avalanche of wild horses. And generally they caught glimpses of a great black branded stallion who led the marauders at such a pace that he seemed almost to fly through the air.

This stallion came to be known as Black Eagle, and to be thoroughly feared and hated from one end of the cattle country to the other. The Bar L ranch appeared to be the heaviest loser. Time after time were its picketed mares run off, again and again were the Bar L herds scattered by the dash of this mysterious band. Was it that Black Eagle could take revenge? Cattlemen have queer notions. They put a price on his head. It was worth six months wages to any cowboy who might kill or capture Black Eagle.

About this time Lefty, the silent man of the Bar L outfit, disappeared. Weeks went by and still the branded stallion remained free and unhurt, for no cow horse in all the West could keep him in sight half an hour.

Black Eagle had been the outlaw king of the ranges for nearly two years when one day, as he was standing at lookout while the band cropped the rich mesa grass behind him, he saw entering the cleft end of a distant arroyo a lone cowboy mounted on a dun little pony. With quick intelligence the stallion noted that this arroyo wound about until its mouth gave upon the side of the mesa not a hundred yards from where he stood.

Promptly did Black Eagle act. Calling his band he led it at a sharp pace to a sheltered hollow on the mesa's back slope. There he left it and hurried away to take up his former position. He had not waited long before the cowboy, riding stealthily, reappeared at the arroyo's mouth. Instantly the race was on. Tossing his fine head in the air and switching haughtily his splendid tail, Black Eagle laid his course in a direction which took him away from his sheltered band. Pounding along behind came the cowboy, urging to utmost endeavor the tough little mustang which he rode.

Had this been simply a race it would have lasted but a short time. But it was more than a race. It was a conflict of strategists. Black Eagle wished to do more than merely out-distance his enemy. He meant to lead him far away and then, under cover of night, return to his band.

Also the cowboy had a purpose. Well knowing that he could neither overtake nor tire the black stallion, he intended to

ride him down by circling. In circling,
the pursuer rides toward the pursued
from an angle, gradually forcing his
quarry into a circular course whose diam-
eter narrows with every turn.

This, however, was a trick Black Eagle
had long ago learned to block. Sure of
his superior speed he galloped away in a
line straight as an arrow's flight, paying
no heed at all to the manner in which he
was followed. Before midnight he had
rejoined his band, while far off on the
prairie was a lone cowboy moodily frying
bacon over a sage-brush fire.

But this pursuer was no faint heart.
Late the next day he was sighted creep-
ing cunningly up to windward. Again
there was a race, not so long this time, for
the day was far spent, but with the same
result.

When for the third time there came
into view this same lone cowboy, Black

Eagle was thoroughly aroused to the fact that this persistent rider meant mischief. Having once more led the cowboy a long and fruitless chase the great black gathered up his band and started south. Not until noon of the next day did he halt, and then only because many of the mares were in bad shape. For a week the band was moved on. During intervals of rest a sharp lookout was kept. Watering places, where an enemy might lurk, were approached only after the most careful scouting.

Despite all caution, however, the cowboy finally appeared on the horizon. Unwilling to endanger the rest of the band, and perhaps wishing a free hand in coping with this evident Nemesis, Black Eagle cantered boldly out to meet him. Just beyond gun range the stallion turned sharply at right angles and sped off over the prairie.

BLACK EAGLE

There followed a curious chase. Day
after day the great black led his pursuer
on, stopping now and then to graze or
take water, never allowing him to cross
the danger line, but never leaving him
wholly out of sight. It was a course of
many windings which Black Eagle took,
now swinging far to the west to avoid a
ranch, now circling east along a water-
course, again doubling back around the
base of a mesa, but in the main going
steadily northward. Up past the brown
Maricopas they worked, across the turgid
Gila, skirting Lone Butte desert; up, up
and on until in the distance glistened the
bald peaks of Silver range.

Never before did a horse play such a
dangerous game, and surely none ever
showed such finesse. Deliberately trailing
behind him an enemy bent on taking
either his life or freedom, not for a moment did Black Eagle show more than

imperative caution. At the close of each day when, by a few miles of judicious gal-loping, he had fully winded the cowboy's mount, the sagacious black would circle to the rear of his pursuer and often, in the gloom of early night, walk recklessly near to the camp of his enemy just for the sake of sniffing curiously. But each morning, as the cowboy cooked his scant breakfast, he would see, standing a few hundred rods away, Black Eagle, pa-tiently waiting for the chase to be re-sumed.

Day after day was the hunted black called upon to foil a new ruse. Some-times it was a game of hide and seek among the buttes, and again it was an early morning sally by the cowboy.

Once during a mid-day stop the dun mustang was turned out to graze. Black Eagle followed suit. A half mile to windward he could see the cow pony, and beside it, evidently sitting with his back toward his quarry, the cowboy. For a half hour, perhaps, all was peace and serenity. Then, as a cougar springing from his lair, there blazed out of the bushes on the bank of a dry water-course to leeward a rifle shot.

Black Eagle felt a shock that stretched him on the grass. There arrived a stinging at the top of his right shoulder and a numbing sensation all along his backbone. Madly he struggled to get on his feet, but he could do no more than raise his fore quarters on his knees. As he did so he saw running toward him from the bushes, coatless and hatless, his relentless pursuer. Black Eagle had been tricked. The figure by the distant mustang then, was only a dummy. He had been shot from ambush. Human strategy had won.

With one last desperate effort, which

sent the red blood spurting from the bullet hole in his shoulder, Black Eagle heaved
himself up until he sat on his haunches,
braced by his forefeet set wide apart.

Then, just as the cowboy brought his
rifle into position for the finishing shot,
the stallion threw up his handsome head,
his big eyes blazing like two stars, and
looked defiantly at his enemy.

Slowly, steadily the cowboy took aim
at the sleek black breast behind which
beat the brave heart of the wild thoroughbred. With finger touching the trigger
he glanced over the sights and looked into
those big, bold eyes. For a full minute
man and horse faced each other thus.
Then the cowboy, in an uncertain, hesi-
tating manner, lowered his rifle. Calmly
Black Eagle waited. But the expected
shot never came. Instead, the cowboy
walked cautiously toward the wounded
stallion.

No move did Black Eagle make, no fear did he show. With a splendid indifference worthy of a martyr he sat there, paying no more heed to his approaching enemy than to the red stream which trickled down his shoulder. He was helpless and knew it, but his noble courage was unshaken. Even when the man came close enough to examine the wound and pat the shining neck that for three years had known neither touch of hand nor bridle-rein, the great stallion did no more than follow with curious, steady gaze.

It is an odd fact that a feral horse, although while free even wilder and fiercer than those native to the prairies, when once returned to captivity resumes almost instantly the traits and habits of domesticity. So it was with Black Eagle. With no more fuss than he would have made when he was a colt in paddock he allowed the cowboy to wash and dress his

wounded shoulder and to lead him about
by the halter.

By a little stream that rounded the base
of a big butte, Lefty—for it was he—
made camp, and every day for a week he
applied to Black Eagle's shoulder a fresh
poultice of pounded cactus leaves. In
that time the big stallion and the silent
man buried distrust and hate and enmity.
No longer were they captive and captor.
They came nearer to being congenial com-
rades than anything else, for in the calm
solitudes of the vast plains such sentiments may thrive.

So, when the wound was fully healed,
the black permitted himself to be bridled
and saddled. With the cow pony following as best it might they rode toward
Santa Fé.

With Black Eagle's return to the
cramped quarters of peopled places there
came experiences entirely new to him.

BLACK EAGLE

Every morning he was saddled by Lefty
and ridden around a fence-enclosed course.
At first he was allowed to set his own gait,
but gradually he was urged to show his
speed. This was puzzling but not a little
to his liking. Also he enjoyed the oats
twice a day and the careful grooming after
each canter. He became accustomed to
stall life and to the scent and voices of
men about him, although as yet he trusted
none but Lefty. Ever kind and consid-
erate he had found Lefty. There were
times, of course, when Black Eagle longed
to be again on the prairie at the head of
his old band, but the joy of circling the
track almost made up for the loss of those
wild free dashes.

One day when Lefty took him out
Black Eagle found many other horses on
the track, while around the enclosure he
saw gathered row on row of men and
women. A band was playing and flags

were snapping in the breeze. There was a thrill of expectation in the air. Black Eagle felt it, and as he pranced proudly down the track there was lifted a murmur of applause and appreciation which made his nerves tingle strangely.

Just how it all came about the big stallion did not fully understand at the time. He heard a bell ring sharply, heard also the shouts of men, and suddenly found himself flying down the course in company with a dozen other horses and riders. They had finished half the circle before Black Eagle fully realized that a gaunt, long-barrelled bay was not only leading him but gaining with every leap. Tossing his black mane in the wind, opening his bright nostrils and pointing his thin, close-set ears forward he swung into the long prairie stride which he was wont to use when leading his wild band. A half dozen leaps brought him abreast the gaunt

bay, and then, feeling Lefty's knees press-
ing his shoulders and hearing Lefty's voice
whispering words of encouragement in
his ears, Black Eagle dashed ahead to
rush down through the lane of frantically
shouting spectators, winner by a half
dozen lengths.

That was the beginning of Black Eagle's
racing career. How it progressed, how he
won races and captured purses in a seemingly endless string of victories unmarred
by a single defeat, that is part of the turf
records of the South and West.

There had to be an end, of course.
Owners of carefully bred running horses
took no great pleasure, you may imagine,
in seeing so many rich prizes captured by
a half-wild branded stallion of no known
pedigree, and ridden by a silent, square-
jawed cowboy. So they sent East for a
"ringer." He came from Chicago in a
box-car with two grooms and he was

entered as an unknown, although in the betting ring the odds posted were one to five on the stranger. Yet it was a grand race. This alleged unknown, with a suppressed record of victories at Sheepshead, Bennings, and The Fort, did no more than shove his long nose under the wire a bare half head in front of Black Eagle's foam-flecked muzzle.

It was sufficient. The once wild stallion knew when he was beaten. He had done his best and he had lost. His high pride had been humbled, his fierce spirit broken. No more did the course hold for him any pleasure, no more could he be thrilled by the cries of spectators or urged into his old time stride by Lefty's whispered appeals. Never again did Black Eagle win a race.

His end, however, was not wholly inglorious. Much against his will the cowboy who had so relentlessly followed Black

BLACK EAGLE

Eagle half way across the big territory of Arizona to lay him low with a rifle bullet, who had spared his life at the last moment and who had ridden him to victory in so many glorious races—this silent, square-jawed man had given him a final caress and then, saying a husky good-by, had turned him over to the owner of a great stud-farm and gone away with a thick roll of bank-notes in his pocket and a guilty feeling in his breast.

Thus it happens that to-day throughout the Southwest there are many black-pointed fleet-footed horses in whose veins runs the blood of a noble horse. Some of them you will find in well-guarded pad-docks, while some still roam the prairies in wild bands which are the menace of stockmen and the vexation of cowboys. As for their sire, he is no more.

This is the story of Black Eagle. Although some of the minor details may be open to dispute, the main points you may hear recited by any cattleman or horse-breeder west of Omaha. For Black Eagle really lived and, as perhaps you will agree, lived not in vain.

BONFIRE

BROKEN FOR THE HOUSE OF JERRY

BONFIRE

BROKEN FOR THE HOUSE OF JERRY

I

DOWN in Maine or up in Vermont, anywhere, in fact, save on a fancy stud-farm, his color would have passed for sorrel. Being a high-bred hackney, and the pick of the Sir Bardolph three-year-olds, he was put down as a strawberry roan. Also he was the pride of Lochlynne.

" 'Osses, women, and the weather, sir, ain't to be depended on; but, barrin' haccidents, that 'ere Bonfire'll fetch us a ribbon if any does, sir." Hawkins, the stud-groom, made this prophecy, not in haste or out of hand, but as one who has

[215]

a reputation to maintain and who speaks
by the card.

So the word was passed among the
under-grooms and stable-boys that Bonfire
was the best of the Sir Bardolph get, and
that he was going to the Garden for the
honor and profit of the farm.

Well, Bonfire had come to the Garden.
He had been there two days. It was
within a few hours of the time when the
hackneys were to take the ring—and look
at him! His eyes were dull, his head was
down, his nostrils wept, his legs trembled.

About his stall was gathered a little
group of discouraged men and boys who
spoke in low tones and gazed gloomily
through the murky atmosphere at the
blanket-swathed, hooded figure that
seemed about to collapse on the straw.

" 'E ain't got no more life in 'im than a
sick cat," said one. " The Bellair folks

will beat us 'oller; every one o' their blooming hentries is as fit as fiddles."

" Ain't we worked on 'im for four mortal hours ? " demanded another. " Wot more can we do ? "

" Send for old 'Awkins an' tell 'im, that's all."

A shudder seemed to shake the group in the stall. It was clear that Mr. Hawkins would be displeased, and that his displeasure was something to be dreaded. Bonfire, too, was seen to shudder, but it was not from fear of Hawkins's wrath. Little did Bonfire care just then for grooms, head or ordinary. He shuddered because of certain aches that dwelt within him.

In his stomach was a queer feeling which he did not at all understand. In his head was a dizziness which made him wish that the stall would not move about so. Streaks of pain shot along his backbone and slid down his legs. Hot and cold flashes swept over his body. For Bonfire had a bad case of car-sickness—a malady differing from sea-sickness largely in name only—also a well-developed cold complicated by nervous indigestion.

Tuned to the key, he had left the home stables. Then they had led him into that box on wheels and the trouble had begun. Men shouted, bells clanged, whistles shrieked. Bonfire felt the box start with a jerk, and, thumping, rumbling, jolting, swaying, move somewhere off into the night.

In an agony of apprehension—neck stretched, eyes staring, ears pointed, nostrils quivering, legs stiffened, Bonfire waited for the end. But of end there seemed to be none. Shock after shock Bonfire withstood, and still found himself waiting. What it all meant he could not guess. There were the other horses that had been taken with him into the box, some placidly munching hay, others looking curiously about. There were the familiar grooms who talked soothingly in his ear and patted his neck in vain. The terror of the thing, this being whirled noisily away in a box, had struck deep into Bonfire's brain, and he could not get it out. So he stood for many hours, neither eating nor sleeping, listening to the noises, feeling the motion, and trembling as one with ague.

Of course it was absurd for Bonfire to go to pieces in that fashion. You can ship a Missouri Modoc around the world and he will finish almost as sound as he started. But Bonfire had blood and breeding and a pedigree which went back to Lady Alice of Burn Brae, Yorkshire.

His coltdom had been a sort of hothouse existence; for Lochlynne, you know, is the toy of a Pennsylvania coal baron, who breeds hackneys, not for profit, but for the joy there is in it; just as other men grow orchids and build cup defenders. At the Lochlynne stables they turn on the steam heat in November. On rainy days you are exercised in a glass-roofed tan-bark ring, and hour after hour you are handled over deep straw to improve your action. You breathe outdoor air only in high-fenced grass paddocks around which you are driven in surcingle rig by a Cockney groom imported with the pigskin saddles and British condition powders. From the day your name is written in the stud-book until you leave, you have balanced feed, all-wool blankets, fly-nettings, and coddling that never ceases. Yet this is the method that rounds you into perfect hackney form.

All this had been done for Bonfire and with apparent success, but a few hours of railroad travel had left him with a set of

nerves as tensely strung as those of a
high-school girl on graduation-day. That
is why a draught of cold air had chilled
him to the bone; that is why, after reaching the Garden, he had gone as limp as a
cut rose at a ball.

II

HAWKINS, who had jumped into his
clothes and hurried to the scene from a
nearby hotel, behaved disappointingly.
He cursed no one, he did not even kick a
stable boy. He just peeled to his under-
shirt and went to work. He stripped
blankets and hood from the wretched
Bonfire, grabbed a bunch of straw in
either hand and began to rub. It was
no chamois polishing. It was a raking,
scraping, rib-bending rub, applied with all
the force in Hawkins's sinewy arms. It
sent the sluggish blood pounding through

every artery of Bonfire's congested system and it made the perspiration ooze from the red face of Hawkins.

At the end of forty minutes' work Bonfire half believed he had been skinned alive. But he had stopped trembling and he held up his head. Next he saw Hawkins shaking something in a thick, long-necked bottle. Suddenly two grooms held Bonfire's jaws apart while Hawkins poured a liquid down his throat. It was fiery stuff that seemed to burn its way, and its immediate effect was to revive Bonfire's appetite.

Hour after hour Hawkins worked and watched the son of Sir Bardolph, and when the get-ready bell sounded he remarked:

"Now, blarst you, we'll see if you're goin' to go to heverlastin' smash in the ring. Tommy, dig out a pair o' them burrs."

Not until he reached the tanbark did Bonfire understand what burrs were.

Then, as a rein was pulled, he felt a hundred sharp points pricking the sensitive skin around his mouth. With a bound he leaped into the ring.

It was a very pretty sight presented to the horse experts lining the rail and to persons in boxes and tier seats. They saw a blockily built strawberry roan, his chiselled neck arched in a perfect crest, his rigid thigh muscles rippling under a shiny coat as he swung his hocks, his slim forelegs sweeping up and out, and every curve of his rounded body, from the tip of his absurd whisk-broom tail to the white snip on the end of his tossing nose, expressing that exuberance of spirits, that jaunty abandon of motion which is the very apex of hackney style. Behind him a short-legged groom bounced through the air at the end of the reins, keeping his feet only by means of most amazing strides.

It was a woman in one of the promenade boxes, a young woman wearing a stunning gown and a preposterous picture-hat, who started the applause. Her hand-clapping was echoed all around the rail, was taken up in the boxes and finally woke a rattling chorus from the crowded tiers above. The three judges, men with whips and long-tailed coats, looked earnestly at the strawberry roan.

Bonfire heard, too, but vaguely. There was a ringing in his ears. Flashes of light half blinded his eyes. The concoction from the long-necked bottle was doing its work. Also the jaw-stinging burrs kept his mind busy. On he danced in a mad effort to escape the pain, and only by careful manœuvring could the grooms get him to stand still long enough for the judges to use the tape.

And when it was all over, after the judges had grouped and regrouped the entries, compared figures and whispered in the ring centre; out of sheer defiance to the preference of the spectators they gave the blue to a chestnut filly with black points—at which the tier seats hissed mightily—and tied a red ribbon to Bonfire's bridle. Thereupon the strawberry roan, who had looked fit for a girth-sling three hours before, tossed his head and pranced daintily out of the arena amid a ringing round of applause.

Hardly had Bonfire's docked tail disappeared before the woman in the stunning gown turned eagerly to a man beside her and asked, "Can't I have him, Jerry? He'll be such a perfect cross-mate for Topsy. Please, now."

To be sure Jerry grumbled some, but inside of a quarter of an hour he had found Hawkins and paid the price; a price worthy of Sir Bardolph and quite in keeping with Lochlynne reckonings.

"'E's been car sick an' show sick," said Hawkins warningly, "an' it'll be a good two weeks afore 'e's in proper condition, sir; but you'll find 'im as neat a bit of 'oss flesh as you hever owned, sir."

Nor was Hawkins wrong. When the burrs were taken off and the effect of the doses from the long-necked bottle had died out, Bonfire looked anything but a ribbon-getter. Luckily Mr. Jerry had a coachman who knew his business. Dan was his name, County Antrim his birthplace. He fed Bonfire hot mixtures, he rubbed, he nursed, until he had coaxed the cold out and had quieted the jangled nerves. Then, one crisp December morning, Bonfire, once more in the pink of condition, was hooked up with Topsy to the pole of a shining, rubber-tired brougham and taken around to make the acquaintance of Mrs. Jerry.

"Oh, isn't he a beauty, Dan!" squealed

Mrs. Jerry delightedly, as Bonfire danced
up to the curb. "Isn't he?"

Dan, trained to silence, touched his
hat. Mrs. Jerry patted Bonfire's rounded
quarter, tried to rub his impatient nose
and squandered on him a bewildering
variety of superlatives. Then she was
handed to her seat, the footman swung
up beside Dan, the reins were slackened
and away they whirled toward the Park,
stepping as if they were going over
hurdles.

III

For three years Bonfire had been in
leather and he had found the life far different from the dull routine of coddling
that he had known at the Lochlynne
Farm. There was little monotony about
it, for the Jerrys were no stay-at-homes.
Of his oak-finished stable, with its sanded

floors and plaited straw stall-mats, Bonfire saw almost as little as did Mrs. Jerry
of her white and gold rooms on the
Avenue.

In the morning it would be a trip down
town, where Topsy and Bonfire would
wait before the big stores, watching the
traffic and people, until Mrs. Jerry reappeared. After luncheon they generally
took her through the Park or up and
down the Avenue to teas and receptions.
In the evening they were often harnessed
again to take Mr. and Mrs. Jerry to dinner, theatre, or ball. Late at night they
might be turned out to fetch them home.

What long, cold waits they had, standing in line sometimes for hours, stamping
their hoofs and shivering under heavy
blankets; for a stylish hackney, you
know, must be kept closely clipped, no
matter what the weather. Why, even
Dan, muffled in his big coat and bear-skin

shoulder-cape, was half frozen. But Dan could leave the footman on the box and go to warm himself in the glittering corner saloons, and when he came back it would be the footman's turn. For Topsy and Bonfire there was no such relief. Chilled, tired, and hungry, they must stamp and wait until at last, far down the street, could be heard the shouting of the strong-lunged carriage-caller. When Dan got his number they were quite ready for the homeward dash.

Seeing them come down the street, heads tossing, pole-chains jingling, the crest and monogram of the house of Jerry glistening on quarter cloth and rosette, their polished hoofs seeming barely to touch the asphalt, you might have thought their lot one to be envied. But Bonfire and Topsy knew better.

It was altogether too heavy work for high-bred hackneys, of course. Mr. Jerry pointed this out, but to no use. Mrs. Jerry asked pertinently what good horses were for if not to be used. No, she wanted no livery teams for the night work. When she rode she wished to ride behind Topsy and Bonfire. They were her horses, anyway. She would do as she pleased. And she did.

Summer brought neither rest nor relief. Early in July horses, servants, and carriages would be shipped off to Newport or Saratoga, there to begin again the unceasing whirl. And fly time, to a dock-tailed horse, is a season of torment.

Of Mrs. Jerry, who had once roused the Garden for his sake, Bonfire caught but glimpses. After that first day, when he was a novelty, he heard no more compliments, received no more pats from her gloved hands. But of slight or neglect Bonfire knew nothing. He curved his neck and threw his hoofs high, whether his muscles ached or no ; in winter he stamped to keep warm, in summer to dislodge the flies; he did his work faithfully, early or late, in cold and in heat ; and all this because he was a son of Sir Bardolph and for the reason that it was his nature to. Had it been put upon him he would have worked in harness until he dropped, prancing his best to the last.

No supreme test, however, was ever brought to the endurance and willingness of Bonfire. They just kept him on the pole, nerves tense, muscles strained, until he began to lose form. His action no longer had that grace and abandon which so pleased Mrs. Jerry when she first saw him. Long standing in the cold numbs the muscles. It robs the legs of their spring. Sudden starts, such as are made when you are called from line after an hour's waiting, finish the business. Try as he might, Bonfire could not step so high, could not carry a perfect crest. His neck had lost its roundness, in his rump a crease had appeared.

To Dan also, came tribulation of his own making. He carried a flat brown flask under the box and there were times when his driving was more a matter of muscular habit than of mental acuteness. Twice he was threatened with discharge and twice he solemnly promised reform. At last the inevitable happened. Dan came one morning to Bonfire's stall, very sober and very sad. He patted Bonfire and said good-by. Then he disappeared.

Less than a week later two young hackneys, plump of neck, round of quarter, springy of knee and hock, were brought to the stable. Bonfire and Topsy were led out of their old stalls to return no more. They had been worn out in the service and cast aside like a pair of old gloves.

BONFIRE

Then did Bonfire enter upon a period of existence in which box-stalls, crested quarter blankets, rubber-tired wheels and liveried drivers had no part. It was a varied existence, filled with toil and hardship and abuse; an existence for which the coddling one gets at Lochlynne Farm is no fit preparation.

IV

JUST where Broadway crosses Sixth Avenue at Thirty-third Street is to be found a dingy, triangular little park plot in which a few gas-stunted, smoke-stained trees make a brave attempt to keep alive. On two sides of the triangle surface-cars whirl restlessly, while overhead the elevated trains rattle and shriek. This part of the metropolis knows little difference between day and night, for the cars never cease, the arc-lights blaze from dusk until dawn and the pavements are never wholly empty.

Locally the section is sometimes called "the Cabman's Graveyard." During any hour of the twenty-four you may find waiting along the curb a line of public carriages. By day you will sometimes see smartly kept hansoms, well-groomed horses, and drivers in neat livery.

But at night the character of the line changes. The carriages are mostly one-horse closed cabs, rickety as to wheels, with torn and faded cushions, license numbers obscured by various devices and rate-cards always missing. The horses are dilapidated, too ; and the drivers, whom you will generally find nodding on the box or sound asleep inside their cabs, harmonize with their rigs.

These are the Nighthawkers of the Tenderloin. The name is not an assur-

ing one, but it is suspected that it has
been aptly given.

One bleak midnight in late November
a cab of this description waited in the lee
of the elevated stairs. The cab itself was
weather-beaten, scratched, and battered.
The driver, who sat half inside and half
outside the vehicle, with his feet on the
sidewalk and his back propped against
the seat-cushion, puffed a short pipe and
watched with indolent but discriminating
eye those who passed. He wore a coachman's coat of faded green which seemed
to have acquired a stain for every button
it had lost. On his head sat jauntily a
rusty beaver and his face, especially the
nose, was of a rich crimson hue.

The horse, that seemed to lean on
rather than stand in the patched shafts,
showed many well-defined points and but
few curves. His thin neck was ewed,
there were deep hollows over the eyes,

the number of his ribs was revealed with startling frankness and the sagging of one hind-quarter betrayed a bad leg. His head he held in spiritless fashion on a level with his knees. As if to add a note of irony, his tail had been docked to the regulation of absurd brevity and served only to tag him as one fallen from a more reputable state.

Suddenly, up and across the intersecting thoroughfares, with a sharp clatter of hoofs, rolled a smart closed brougham. The dispirited bobtail looked up as a well-mated pair pranced past. Perhaps he noted their sleek quarters, the glittering trappings on their backs and their gingery action. As he dropped his head again something very like a sigh escaped him. It might have been regret, perhaps it was only a touch of influenza.

The driver, too, saw the turnout and gazed after it. But he did not sigh. He

BONFIRE

puffed away at his pipe as if entirely sat-
isfied with his lot. He was still watching
the brougham when a surface-car came
gliding swiftly around a curve. There
was a smash of splintering wood and
breaking glass. The car had struck the
brougham a battering-ram blow, crushing
a rear wheel and snapping the steel axle
at the hub

From somewhere or other a crowd
of curious persons appeared and circled
about to watch while the driver held the
plunging horses and the footman hauled
from the overturned carriage a man and a
woman in evening dress. The couple
seemed unhurt and, although somewhat
rumpled as to attire, remarkably uncon-
cerned.

" Keb, sir ! Have a keb, sir?"

The Nighthawker was on the scene,
like a longshore wrecker, and waving an
inviting arm toward his shabby vehicle.

[237]

The man coolly restored to shape his misused opera hat, adjusted his necktie, whispered some orders to his coachman and then asked of the Nighthawker: " Where's your carriage, my man? "

Eagerly the green-coated cabby led the way until the rescued couple stood before it. The woman inspected the battered vehicle doubtfully before stepping inside. The man eyed the sorry nag for a moment and then said, with a laugh: "Good frame you have there; got the parts all numbered?"

But the Nighthawker was not sensitive. The intimation that his horse might fall apart he answered only with a good-natured chuckle and asked: " Where shall it be; home, sir? "

" Why, yes, drive us to number——"

" Oh, we know the house well enough, sir, Bonfire and me."

" Bonfire! Bonfire, did you say? " Incredulously the fare looked first at the horse and then at the driver. "Why, 'pon my word, it's old Dan! And this relic in the shafts is Bonfire, is it?"

"It's him, sir; leastways, all there's left of him."

"Well, I'll be hanged! Kitty! Kitty!" he shouted into the cab where my lady was nervously pulling her skirts closer about her and sniffing the tobacco-laden atmosphere with evident disapproval. "Here's Dan, our old coachman."

"Really?" was the unenthusiastic reply from the cab.

"Yes, and he's driving Bonfire. You remember Bonfire, the hackney I bought for you at the Garden the year we were married."

"Indeed? Why, how odd? But do come in, Jerry, and let's get on home. I'm so-o-o-o tired."

Mr. Jerry stifled his sentiment and

shut the cab-door with a bang. Dan pulled Bonfire's head into position and lightly laid the whip over the all too obvious ribs. Bonfire, his head bobbing ludicrously on his thin neck and his stubby tail keeping time at the other end of him, moved uncertainly up the avenue at a jerky hobble.

And there let us leave him. Poor old Bonfire! Bred to win a ribbon at the Garden—ended as the drudge of a Tenderloin Nighthawker.

PASHA

THE SON OF SELIM

PASHA

THE SON OF SELIM

LONG, far too long, has the story of Pasha, son of Selim, remained untold.

The great Selim, you know, was brought from far across the seas, where he had been sold for a heavy purse by a venerable sheik, who tore his beard during the bargain and swore by Allah that without Selim there would be for him no joy in life. Also he had wept quite convincingly on Selim's neck—but he finished by taking the heavy purse. That was how Selim, the great Selim, came to end his days in Fayette County, Kentucky. Of his many sons, Pasha was one.

In almost idyllic manner were spent the years of Pasha's coltdom. They were years of pasture roaming and bluegrass cropping. When the time was ripe, began the hunting lessons. Pasha came to know the feel of the saddle and the voice of the hounds. He was taught the long, easy lope. He learned how to gather himself for a sail through the air over a hurdle or a water-jump. Then, when he could take five bars clean, when he could clear an eight-foot ditch, when his wind was so sound that he could lead the chase from dawn until high noon, he was sent to the stables of a Virginia tobacco-planter who had need of a new hunter and who could afford Arab blood.

In the stalls at Gray Oaks stables were many good hunters, but none better than Pasha. Cream-white he was, from the tip of his splendid, yard-long tail to his pink-lipped muzzle. His coat was as silk plush, his neck as supple as a swan's, and out of his big, bright eyes there looked such intelligence that one half expected him to speak. His lines were all long, graceful curves, and when he danced daintily on his slender legs one could see the muscles flex under the delicate skin.

Miss Lou claimed Pasha for her very own at first sight. As no one at Gray Oaks denied Miss Lou anything at all, to her he belonged from that instant. Of Miss Lou, Pasha approved thoroughly. She knew that bridle-reins were for gentle guidance, not for sawing or jerking, and that a riding-crop was of no use whatever save to unlatch a gate or to cut at an unruly hound. She knew how to rise on the stirrup when Pasha lifted himself in his stride, and how to settle close to the pig-skin when his hoofs hit the ground.

In other words, she had a good seat, which means as much to the horse as it does to the rider.

Besides all this, it was Miss Lou who insisted that Pasha should have the best of grooming, and she never forgot to bring the dainties which Pasha loved, an apple or a carrot or a sugar-plum. It is something, too, to have your nose patted by a soft gloved hand and to have such a person as Miss Lou put her arm around your neck and whisper in your ear. From no other than Miss Lou would Pasha permit such intimacy.

No paragon, however, was Pasha. He had a temper, and his whims were as many as those of a school-girl. He was particular as to who put on his bridle. He had notions concerning the manner in which a currycomb should be used. A red ribbon or a bandanna handkerchief put him in a rage, while green, the holy

color of the Mohammedan, soothed his
nerves. A lively pair of heels he had,
and he knew how to use his teeth. The
black stable-boys found that out, and so
did the stern-faced man who was known
as "Mars" Clayton. This "Mars" Clayton had ridden Pasha once, had ridden
him as he rode his big, ugly, hard-bitted
roan hunter, and Pasha had not enjoyed
the ride. Still, Miss Lou and Pasha often
rode out with "Mars" Clayton and the
parrot-nosed roan. That is, they did
until the coming of Mr. Dave.

In Mr. Dave, Pasha found a new friend.
From a far Northern State was Mr. Dave.
He had come in a ship to buy tobacco, but
after he had bought his cargo he still
stayed at Gray Oaks, "to complete
Pasha's education," so he said.

Many ways had Mr. Dave which Pasha
liked. He had a gentle manner of talking to you, of smoothing your flanks and

rubbing your ears, which gained your confidence and made you sure that he understood. He was firm and sure in giving commands, yet so patient in teaching one tricks, that it was a pleasure to learn.

So, almost before Pasha knew it, he could stand on his hind legs, could step around in a circle in time to a tune which Mr. Dave whistled, and could do other things which few horses ever learn to do. His chief accomplishment, however, was to kneel on his forelegs in the attitude of prayer. A long time it took Pasha to learn this, but Mr. Dave told him over and over again, by word and sign, until at last the son of the great Selim could strike a pose such as would have done credit to a Mecca pilgrim.

"It's simply wonderful!" declared Miss Lou.

But it was nothing of the sort. Mr.

PASHA

Dave had been teaching tricks to horses ever since he was a small boy, and never had he found such an apt pupil as Pasha.

Many a glorious gallop did Pasha and Miss Lou have while Mr. Dave stayed at Gray Oaks, Dave riding the big bay gelding that Miss Lou, with all her daring, had never ventured to mount. It was not all galloping though, for Pasha and the big bay often walked for miles through the wood lanes, side by side and very close together, while Miss Lou and Mr. Dave talked, talked, talked. How they could ever find so much to say to each other Pasha wondered.

But at last Mr. Dave went away, and with his going ended good times for Pasha, at least for many months. There followed strange doings. There was much excitement among the stable-boys, much riding about, day and night, by the men of Gray Oaks, and no hunting at all.

One day the stables were cleared of all horses save Pasha.

"Some time, if he is needed badly, you may have Pasha, but not now," Miss Lou had said. And then she had hidden her face in his cream-white mane and sobbed. Just what the trouble was Pasha did not understand, but he was certain "Mars" Clayton was at the bottom of it.

No longer did Miss Lou ride about the country. Occasionally she galloped up and down the highway, to the Pointdexters and back, just to let Pasha stretch his legs. Queer sights Pasha saw on these trips. Sometimes he would pass many men on horses riding close together in a pack, as the hounds run when they have the scent. They wore strange clothing, did these men, and they carried, instead of riding-crops, big shiny knives that swung at their sides. The sight of them set Pasha's nerves tingling. He would

sniff curiously after them and then prick
forward his ears and dance nervously.

Of course Pasha knew that something
unusual was going on, but what it was he
could not guess. There came a time,
however, when he found out all about it.
Months had passed when, late one night,
a hard-breathing, foam-splotched, mud-
covered horse was ridden into the yard
and taken into the almost deserted stable.
Pasha heard the harsh voice of " Mars "
Clayton swearing at the stable-boys.
Pasha heard his own name spoken, and
guessed that it was he who was wanted.
Next came Miss Lou to the stable.

"I'm very sorry," he heard "Mars"
Clayton say, "but I've got to get out of
this. The Yanks are not more than five
miles behind."

"But you'll take good care of him,
won't you?" he heard Miss Lou ask
eagerly.

"Oh, yes; of course," replied "Mars" Clayton, carelessly.

A heavy saddle was thrown on Pasha's back, the girths pulled cruelly tight, and in a moment "Mars" Clayton was on his back. They were barely clear of Gray Oaks driveway before Pasha felt something he had never known before. It was as if someone had jabbed a lot of little knives into his ribs. Roused by pain and fright, Pasha reared in a wild attempt to unseat this hateful rider. But "Mars" Clayton's knees seemed glued to Pasha's shoulders. Next Pasha tried to shake him off by sudden leaps, side-bolts, and stiff-legged jumps. These manœuvres brought vicious jerks on the wicked chain-bit that was cutting Pasha's tender mouth sorrily and more jabs from the little knives. In this way did Pasha fight until his sides ran with blood and his breast was plastered thick with reddened foam.

PASHA

In the meantime he had covered miles of road, and at last, along in the cold gray of the morning, he was ridden into a field where were many tents and horses. Pasha was unsaddled and picketed to a stake. This latter indignity he was too much exhausted to resent. All he could do was to stand, shivering with cold, trembling from nervous excitement, and wait for what was to happen next.

It seemed ages before anything did happen. The beginning was a tripping bugle-blast. This was answered by the voice of other bugles blown here and there about the field. In a moment men began to tumble out of the white tents. They came by twos and threes and dozens, until the field was full of them. Fires were built on the ground, and soon Pasha could scent coffee boiling and bacon frying. Black boys began moving about among the horses with hay and oats and water.

One of them rubbed Pasha hurriedly with a wisp of straw. It was little like the currying and rubbing with brush and comb and flannel to which he was accustomed and which he needed just then, oh, how sadly. His strained muscles had stiffened so much that every movement gave him pain. So matted was his coat with sweat and foam and mud that it seemed as if half the pores of his skin were choked.

He had cooled his parched throat with a long draught of somewhat muddy water, but he had eaten only half of the armful of hay when again the bugles sounded and "Mars" Clayton appeared. Tightening the girths, until they almost cut into Pasha's tender skin, he jumped into the saddle and rode off to where a lot of big black horses were being reined into line. In front of this line Pasha was wheeled. He heard the bugles sound once more, heard his rider shout something to the men behind, felt the wicked little knives in his sides, and then, in spite of aching legs, was forced into a sharp gallop. Although he knew it not, Pasha had joined the Black Horse Cavalry.

The months that followed were to Pasha one long, ugly dream. Not that he minded the hard riding by day and night. In time he became used to all that. He could even endure the irregular feeding, the sleeping in the open during all kinds of weather, and the lack of proper grooming. But the vicious jerks on the torture-provoking cavalry bit, the flat sabre blows on the flank which he not infrequently got from his ill-tempered master, and, above all, the cruel digs of the spur-wheels—these things he could not understand. Such treatment he was sure he did not merit. "Mars" Clayton he came to hate more and more. Some day, Pasha told himself, he would take vengeance with teeth and heels, even if he died for it.

In the meantime he had learned the cavalry drill. He came to know the meaning of each varying bugle-call, from reveille, when one began to paw and stamp for breakfast, to mournful taps, when lights went out, and the tents became dark and silent. Also, one learned to slow from a gallop into a walk; when to wheel to the right or to the left, and when to start on the jump as the first notes of a charge were sounded. It was better to learn the bugle-calls, he found, than to wait for a jerk on the bits or a prod from the spurs.

No more was he terror-stricken, as he had been on his first day in the cavalry, at hearing behind him the thunder of many hoofs. Having once become used to the noise, he was even thrilled by the swinging metre of it. A kind of wild harmony was in it, something which made one forget everything else. At such times Pasha longed to break into his long, wind-splitting lope, but he learned that he must leave the others no more than a pace or two behind, although he could have easily outdistanced them all.

Also, Pasha learned to stand under fire. No more did he dance at the crack of carbines or the zipp-zipp of bullets. He could even hold his ground when shells went screaming over him, although this was hardest of all to bear. One could not see them, but their sound, like that of great birds in flight, was something to try one's nerves. Pasha strained his ears to catch the note of each shell that came whizzing overhead, and, as it passed, looked inquiringly over his shoulder as if to ask, " Now what on earth was that ? "

But all this experience could not pre-

pare him for the happenings of that never-
to-be-forgotten day in June. There had
been a period full of hard riding and ending with a long halt. For several days
hay and oats were brought with some regularity. Pasha was even provided with
an apology for a stall. It was made by
leaning two rails against a fence. Some
hay was thrown between the rails. This
was a sorry substitute for the roomy box-
stall, filled with clean straw, which Pasha
always had at Gray Oaks, but it was as
good as any provided for the Black Horse
Cavalry.

And how many, many horses there
were ! As far as Pasha could see in either
direction the line extended. Never before
had he seen so many horses at one time.
And men ! The fields and woods were
full of them ; some in brown butternut,
some in homespun gray, and many in
clothes having no uniformity of color at

all. " Mars " Clayton was dressed better than most, for on his butternut coat were shiny shoulder-straps, and it was closed with shiny buttons. Pasha took little pride in this. He knew his master for a cruel and heartless rider, and for nothing more.

One day there was a great parade, when Pasha was carefully groomed for the first time in months. There were bands playing and flags flying. Pasha, forgetful of his ill-treatment and prancing proudly at the head of a squadron of coal-black horses, passed in review before a big, bearded man wearing a slouch hat fantastically decorated with long plumes and sitting a great black horse in the midst of a little knot of officers.

Early the next morning Pasha was awakened by the distant growl of heavy guns. By daylight he was on the move, thousands of other horses with him.

Nearer and nearer they rode to the place where the guns were growling. Sometimes they were on roads, sometimes they crossed fields, and again they plunged into the woods where the low branches struck one's eyes and scratched one's flanks. At last they broke clear of the trees to come suddenly upon such a scene as Pasha had never before witnessed.

Far across the open field he could see troop on troop of horses coming toward him. They seemed to be pouring over the crest of a low hill, as if driven onward by some unseen force behind. Instantly Pasha heard, rising from the throats of thousands of riders, on either side and behind him, that fierce, wild yell which he had come to know meant the approach of trouble. High and shrill and menacing it rang as it was taken up and repeated by those in the rear. Next the bugles began to sound, and in quick obedience the horses formed in line just on the edge of the woods, a line which stretched and stretched on either flank until one could hardly see where it ended.

From the distant line came no answering cry, but Pasha could hear the bugles blowing and he could see the fronts massing. Then came the order to charge at a gallop. This set Pasha to tugging eagerly at the bit, but for what reason he did not know. He knew only that he was part of a great and solid line of men and horses sweeping furiously across a field toward that other line which he had seen pouring over the hill-crest.

He could scarcely see at all now. The thousands of hoofs had raised a cloud of dust that not only enveloped the onrushing line, but rolled before it. Nor could Pasha hear anything save the thunderous thud of many feet. Even the shrieking of the shells was drowned. But for the re-

straining bit Pasha would have leaped forward and cleared the line. Never had he
been so stirred. The inherited memory
of countless desert raids, made by his
Arab ancestors, was doing its work. For
what seemed a long time this continued,
and then, in the midst of the blind and
frenzied race, there loomed out of the
thick air, as if it had appeared by magic,
the opposing line.

Pasha caught a glimpse of something
which seemed like a heaving wall of tossing heads and of foam-whitened necks
and shoulders. Here and there gleamed
red, distended nostrils and straining eyes.
Bending above was another wall, a wall
of dusty blue coats, of grim faces, and of
dust-powdered hats. Bristling above all
was a threatening crest of waving blades.

What would happen when the lines
met? Almost before the query was
thought there came the answer. With

an earth-jarring crash they came together.
The lines wavered back from the shock
of impact and then the whole struggle
appeared to Pasha to centre about him.
Of course this was not so. But it was a
fact that the most conspicuous figure in
either line had been that of the cream-
white charger in the very centre of the
Black Horse regiment.

For one confused moment Pasha heard
about his ears the whistle and clash of
sabres, the spiteful crackle of small arms,
the snorting of horses, and the cries of
men. For an instant he was wedged
tightly in the frenzied mass, and then, by
one desperate leap, such as he had learned
on the hunting field, he shook himself clear.

Not until some minutes later did Pasha
notice that the stirrups were dangling
empty and that the bridle-rein hung loose
on his neck. Then he knew that at
last he was free from "Mars" Clayton.

At the same time he felt himself seized by an overpowering dread. While conscious of a guiding hand on the reins Pasha had abandoned himself to the fierce joy of the charge. But now, finding himself riderless in the midst of a horrid din, he knew not what to do, nor which way to turn. His only impulse was to escape. But where? Lifting high his fine head and snorting with terror he rushed about, first this way and then that, frantically seeking a way out of this fog-filled field of dreadful pandemonium. Now he swerved in his course to avoid a charging squad, now he was turned aside by prone objects at sight of which he snorted fearfully. Although the blades still rang and the carbines still spoke, there were no more to be seen either lines or order. Here and there in the dust-clouds scurried horses, some with riders and some without, by twos, by fours, or in squads of twenty or more. The sound of shooting and slashing and shouting filled the air.

To Pasha it seemed an eternity that he had been tearing about the field when he shied at the figure of a man sitting on the ground. Pasha was about to wheel and dash away when the man called to him. Surely the tones were familiar. With wide-open, sniffing nostrils and trembling knees, Pasha stopped and looked hard at the man on the ground.

"Pasha! Pasha!" the man called weakly. The voice sounded like that of Mr. Dave.

"Come, boy! Come, boy!" said the man in a coaxing tone, which recalled to Pasha the lessons he had learned at Gray Oaks years before. Still Pasha sniffed and hesitated.

"Come here, Pasha, old fellow. For God's sake, come here!"

There was no resisting this appeal. Step by step Pasha went nearer. He continued to tremble, for this man on the ground, although his voice was that of Mr. Dave, looked much different from the one who had taught him tricks. Besides, there was about him the scent of fresh blood. Pasha could see the stain of it on his blue trousers.

"Come, boy. Come, Pasha," insisted the man on the ground, holding out an encouraging hand. Slowly Pasha obeyed until he could sniff the man's fingers. Another step and the man was smoothing his nose, still speaking gently and coaxingly in a faint voice. In the end Pasha was assured that the man was really the Mr. Dave of old, and glad enough Pasha was to know it.

"Now, Pasha," said Mr. Dave, "we'll see if you've forgotten your tricks, and may the good Lord grant you haven't. Down, sir! Kneel, Pasha, kneel!"

"Come, boy. Come, Pasha," insisted the man on the ground.

PASHA

It had been a long time since Pasha
had been asked to do this, a very long
time; but here was Mr. Dave asking him,
in just the same tone as of old, and in just
the same way. So Pasha, forgetting his
terror under the soothing spell of Mr.
Dave's voice, forgetting the fearful sights
and sounds about him, remembering only
that here was the Mr. Dave whom he
loved, asking him to do his old trick—
well, Pasha knelt.

"Easy now, boy; steady!" Pasha
heard him say. Mr. Dave was dragging
himself along the ground to Pasha's side.
"Steady now, Pasha; steady, boy!" He
felt Mr. Dave's hand on the pommel.
"So-o-o, boy; so-o-o-o!" Slowly, oh,
so slowly, he felt Mr. Dave crawling into
the saddle, and although Pasha's knees
ached from the unfamiliar strain, he stirred
not a muscle until he got the command,
"Up, Pasha, up!"

[267]

Then, with a trusted hand on the
bridle-rein, Pasha joyfully bounded away
through the fog, until the battle-field was
left behind. Of the long ride that ensued
only Pasha knows, for Mr. Dave kept his
seat in the saddle more by force of muscular habit than anything else. A man
who has learned to sleep on horseback
does not easily fall off, even though he
has not the full command of his senses.
Only for the first hour or so did Pasha's
rider do much toward guiding their
course. In hunting-horses, however, the
sense of direction is strong. Pasha had
it—especially for one point of the com-
pass. This point was south. So, un-
knowing of the possible peril into which
he might be taking his rider, south he
went. How Pasha ever did it, as I have
said, only Pasha knows; but in the end
he struck the Richmond Pike.

It was a pleading whinny which aroused

Mr. Dave kept his seat in the saddle more by force of muscular
habit than anything else.

PASHA

Miss Lou at early daybreak. Under her window she saw Pasha, and on his back a limp figure in a blue, dust-covered, dark-stained uniform. And that was how Pasha's cavalry career came to an end. That one fierce charge was his last.

.   .   .   .

In the Washington home of a certain Maine Congressman you may see, hung in a place of honor and lavishly framed, the picture of a horse. It is very creditably done in oils, is this picture. It is of a cream-white horse, with an arched neck, clean, slim legs, and a splendid flowing tail.

Should you have any favors of state to ask of this Maine Congressman, it would be the wise thing, before stating your request, to say something nice about the horse in the picture. Then the Congressman will probably say, looking fondly at the picture: "I must tell Lou—er—my

[269]

wife, you know, what you have said. Yes, that was Pasha. He saved my neck at Brandy Station. He was one-half Arab, Pasha was, and the other half, sir, was human."